D1258876

THE TRUEST HOME

ALASKAN HEARTS, BOOK 3

MELISSA STORM

Editor: Megan Harris
Proofreaders: Jasmine Bryner
Cover by Daqri Bernardo at Covers by Combs

Partridge & Pear Press

PO Box 72

Brighton, MI 48116

To my father-in-law, Mark S.
For accepting a damaged, little boy and raising him into
the man I love.

Liz Benjamin has lost her place in the world. Not only are her best friends too busy for her, but her father just married a horrible woman who has now moved into their home with her two horrible daughters.

Worse still, a handsome stranger arrives in town for the wedding and starts asking all the wrong questions. With his help, Liz soon finds that everything she thought she knew about herself is based on a terrible lie.

But just how far back does the deception go, and how will finding the truth about Liz's past change her future?

Join Liz, Scarlett, Lauren, and their courageous team of sled dogs in this unforgettable tale of tenacity, trust, and finding where you belong. Start reading THE TRUEST HOME today!

AUTHOR'S NOTE

I must've started and stopped writing this afterword a dozen times. Due to the nature of this book and the fact she chose to dedicate it to my dad, Mrs. Storm asked me to write something about fatherhood. I've come to the conclusion that it's a lot harder to describe than you might think, because I think it takes something truly special to be a real dad.

When Mrs. Storm was pregnant with our daughter, I was terrified. What type of father would I end up being? Every night, I lay awake wondering if I would end up like my abuser instead of like a father. You see, for ten years, I lived in hell, being physically abused by my stepfather. I was suicidal at the age of 8. I was severely introverted and preferred to be alone than around people. I had a temper. I had panic attacks. I dabbled in self-harm. I allowed myself to be abused by people well into adulthood. How was someone as messed up as me supposed to be a father to another human being?

But if my stepfather was the devil that I feared becoming, I luckily had my dad to strive to be like. He has three children, and even if we aren't all genetically linked, we are all bound by his love. My dad loves unconditionally, in a way that seems alien in today's world. And for him to take me at sixteen, at my most obnoxious, rebellious, and broken, and still find a way to help me... I don't think there are words to really describe it. For me, everything I could strive to be as a father was embodied by my dad.

And the biggest lesson I learned was one that I'm still learning today. Nobody's perfect. We all make mistakes. But the perfect father can acknowledge these flaws in himself and strive to do the very best for their child. Sometimes that can be tough love. Sometimes that can be a kind word at a low point. Sometimes it's just stepping back and allowing your children to make their own mistakes.

Thank you, Dad, for all you taught me. For all the patience you showed me. And, most of all, for loving this broken boy and teaching him to be a father to your granddaughter.

CHAPTER 1

LIZ BENJAMIN TRIED TO SMILE AS SHE WALKED DOWN THE petal-strewn aisle toward her father.

He beamed as she moved closer, his expression an unfamiliar mix of nervousness, euphoria, and even pride. This was his special day, and Liz wanted it to be perfect for him...

Even though he was marrying the Wicked Witch of West Anchorage.

As much as Liz despised her soon-to-be stepmother, Vanessa Price, she knew well enough that you couldn't choose who your heart loved. She'd seen that lesson firsthand as her best friend—and now roommate—Scarlett Cole fell head over heels for the heir to the infamous Mitchell estate.

From her seat in the pew, Scarlett gave a thumbs up as Liz passed by on her long walk toward the front of the church. Her new fiancé Henry sat by her side, his fingers laced possessively through hers.

After a couple false starts, Henry had proven himself to be a good man. He had taught both Scarlett and Liz many lessons in their short friendship. For one thing, appearances could be deceiving. And, more importantly than that, a person isn't necessarily destined to follow in his family's footsteps.

Henry certainly hadn't.

And that's what Liz reminded herself often when it came to her new stepsisters, Victoria and Valeria, who would soon follow her down the aisle. Sure, their mother was the very caricature of an evil, money-grubbing politician, but that didn't mean her daughters weren't lovely people in their own right.

When the two families had first met, the two high school girls had kept mostly to themselves, rebuffing any attempt Liz made to hold a conversation. But that could be immaturity—or even shyness—just as much as it could be a cold nature.

Although...

No, Liz had to give them the benefit of the doubt—both for her own sanity and her father's.

As far as she knew, he hadn't gone on a single date since the death of her mother more than twenty-five years ago. Not until he'd met and fallen headlong for Vanessa.

Poor Liz had never gotten the chance to know her mother, who had sadly died in childbirth. It was the one thing she wished she could change about her life. Well, other than the way her father had punished himself by swearing off love for so many years.

He had once told Liz he didn't deserve happiness, but hadn't explained when she pressed him for answers. Her entire life it had been just the two of them, but now three more would be entering their family.

She needed to play nice for her father's sake. Surely he must see something in Vanessa Price that Liz herself hadn't spied yet. She couldn't imagine her dear old dad choosing anyone with less than a pure heart to share his life.

But then again, maybe he had been tricked somehow, pulled into Vanessa's black widow web.

Only, what could she possibly have to gain by going after Ben Benjamin?

None of it made sense to Liz. Maybe one day when she finally fell in love for herself, things would start to make more sense. Maybe Vanessa would change, or maybe she already had without Liz's realizing it.

A wedding was a day to be happy, yet the only emotion that filled Liz's heart that day was fear. She still couldn't decide whether she should be happy her father had finally found a partner or sad by just who that partner ended up being.

When all was said and done, would this truly be the happiest day of her father's life?

Oh, how she hoped so. And that hope was what she would cling to in the absence of any more attractive option.

She looked up and smiled, finally having finished her long walk toward the front of the church and taking her place beside her father. She was his best man, though she wore a dress that matched her sisters' bridesmaids gowns.

Victoria and Valeria floated down the aisle next, arms linked, smiling proudly out at the sea of guests. Their perfect blonde ringlets seemed to shine and reflect the light from the many flashing cameras. Their pale blue, floor-length gowns added to the ethereal image they projected.

Liz looked nowhere near as gorgeous in her dress. The color clashed with her thick auburn hair. The low cut of the neckline showed off the freckles she'd prefer to hide and the cleavage which, quite frankly, didn't really exist.

Her new stepsisters were more than ten years younger than her, yet their bra cups runneth over. God may have granted them beauty and money, but Liz knew she was the one who had truly been blessed, having a father like Ben Benjamin.

She had never wanted for anything growing up, and she didn't want for anything now.

Just for him to be happy with the new path he'd chosen.

As the organist played the first few notes of the "Wedding March," all eyes shifted toward the back of the church where Vanessa Price stood wearing layers and layers of white tulle, a wispy veil that reached straight to the floor, and even a tiara embedded with hundreds of tiny crystals.

Everyone watched the bride as she took smooth, delicate steps toward the altar, but Liz couldn't stop looking at the tears that shone in her father's eyes, the impossibly huge smile that somehow managed to grow even larger.

Happy.

He was finally happy.

And she wouldn't let anyone take that away.

CHAPTER 2

Liz looked away as her father kissed his bride, making the union of the Benjamin and Price families official in the eyes of both God and the law.

She held her breath as the couple marched back down the aisle, hand in hand. And she didn't laugh with the other guests when her father leaped up and attempted to click his heels together in glee.

After what felt like an eternity of nodding, smiling, and greeting the guests as they filed through the receiving line, a gleaming black limo came to collect the wedding party and drive them to the banquet hall for the reception.

The reception venue was decorated beautifully, like a scene straight out of a fairytale. A mirrored placemat, glass dish, and crystal goblet adorned each place setting. Even the silverware shone with added bedazzlements on their dainty handles.

An oblong, silver stage rose several feet above the floor with four throne-like chairs set around a thin table. Liz looked back to her father, but he didn't notice her worried expression as he and his bride ascended to the stage and took the two middle seats. The waiting guests clapped and cheered, ready for the next portion of this evening's spectacle.

Next, Valeria and Victoria took their seats on either side of the couple. Finally, her father noticed the missing chair and motioned for Liz to join them on the stage.

"Scooch, scooch," he told Valeria so that they could squeeze in one more place between her and Liz's father. It was an uncomfortably tight fit. Especially since the slight felt intentional. It was crazy to assume that her new stepmother would purposely exclude her, but how could a woman known for her expert organization skills miss something so obvious when planning her own wedding?

It wasn't just the stage arrangement, either.

It was the dresses that clashed with Liz's coloring and build, while perfectly complementing Victoria and Valeria's. It was Vanessa's insistence upon having the wedding on the same day as an important qualifying race for the Iditarod, meaning her new husband would have to be miss out on the officiating duties he so loved. And it was the fact that Liz's shoes—the ones Vanessa had insisted match those of her girls—had been ordered a size too small.

The whole day was terribly uncomfortable for Liz, and yet...

Her father seemed so, so happy.

She smiled, nodded, did whatever she could to be supportive until, at last, the dinner portion of the evening had ended and the band announced the first dance.

Liz flew away from the stage as fast as her aching, pinched feet would carry her and straight over to table thirteen where her best friends, Scarlett and Lauren, sat with the special men in their lives.

"Everything's so nice," Lauren said with a placating smile.

"Yeah, too nice for her," Scarlett grumbled. Her friend and new stepmother had practically come to blows over Vanessa's interference at the library where Scarlett had once worked. Back then, Vanessa had used her strategic budget cuts to drive a wedge between Scarlett and her fiancé, Henry —a wedge that had almost kept them apart for good.

But love always finds a way, Liz reminded herself. Hopefully it would for her father and his new bride as well.

"Be nice." Henry pulled Scarlett to his side and kissed her on the cheek. "I don't like her much, either, but she's Liz's family now. Besides, I'm sure she was under an enormous amount of pressure from her constituents."

"To be fair, she's the one who chose politics in the first place, but sure. Whatever. I'll be nice." Scarlett shook her head and made a silly face, lightening the burden on Liz's heart.

"You look... stressed," Lauren's husband, Shane, said. "Want me to grab you a drink?"

"Good idea. Thanks," Liz answered, realizing just how much a glass of wine might help to quiet her nerves so she could maybe actually enjoy the rest of the evening.

Just then, the band front man announced an open dance floor and invited everyone to come and join the bride and groom for a fun, up-tempo number. Scarlett and Henry exchanged awkward glances, which made Liz wonder if they perhaps were thinking of the night they'd first met at the Miners and Trappers' ball nearly two years ago.

Liz waved her hand at them. "Go. Go dance. All of you. I'll get my own drink and join you in a bit."

Lauren and Scarlett both gave her quick hugs, then led their partners across the hall and onto the dance floor.

Liz had never much been enamored of the idea of love growing up, but now she craved it in a way she hadn't before. Her friends, her father, all the important people in her lives had somebody.

Liz, on the other hand, only had herself.

Well, until a stranger appeared at her side, seemingly out of nowhere. She assumed he was just pausing in his search for someone across the room, but no. He nodded at Liz as he closed the distance between them.

"Liz Benjamin?" he asked, extending his hand toward her. The way his green eyes fixed on her implied he knew exactly who she was, though Liz had never seen this man a day in her life until now.

"Yes? Can I help you?" She was too puzzled by his sudden appearance to remember her manners. She'd already been forcing them all night. Now, she was too tired to care any longer. And her feet hurt too much for her to so much as fake a smile.

The man didn't seem to notice Liz's foul mood, or perhaps he'd been expecting it. His smile remained glued in place as he delivered his next line. "I'm hoping so. My name's Dorian Whitley, and I'm here covering the event for the *Anchorage Daily News.*"

"The event?" She frowned at him, wishing he would just go away. "Is my dad's wedding some political thing now?"

"No, nothing like that. It's for the society page. And I'm still waiting for you to say hello." He chuckled and reached his hand toward her again, waiting until she finally took it in greeting.

"Yes, of course. Hello." She shook his hand once, twice, a third time. Still he didn't loosen his grip. Instead, he tugged her in closer to him.

His green eyes flashed. Liz wondered why the color

reminded her of slime and serpents rather than emeralds or something pleasant. Was she projecting her bad mood onto everyone and everything she encountered, or was her subconscious picking up on something and trying to warn the rest of her?

Dorian smiled again. Smooth. Practiced. Like perhaps he was in a play. "I have some questions. Just little facts I was hoping you could verify for my piece. Mind if I ask you over a dance?"

Liz thought about this for a second. She didn't want to dance, didn't want to spend time with this peculiar man, didn't want to be here at all.

But then again...

Dancing and playing merry could help her blend in better with the rest of the wedding guests. Surely that would make Vanessa happy. The puff piece Dorian planned to write would make her happy, too.

And if Vanessa was happy, Liz's father would be happy.

"Sure, I guess," Liz answered, trying to keep her voice light as she did. She did, however, insist upon one condition. "Mind if I leave my shoes here? My feet are killing me."

CHAPTER 3

Liz sighed with relief as she slid the heels from her feet. The patent leather matched the pale blue of the bridesmaid dresses almost perfectly. The shoes were so shiny they almost appeared to be made of mirrored glass, much like the decorations strung about the hall.

Dorian offered his hand and led her to the dance floor. As far as men were concerned, he was certainly handsome enough. His brown hair lay close to his head in loose curls, the softness of which contrasted greatly with his strong jaw and angular nose. His eyes, which had been the first thing Liz noticed about him, were made up of several shades of green, each of varying intensity. Regardless of their color, Dorian's eyes seemed to hold many unspoken words - questions, perhaps - for his column.

All things considered, Dorian did not fit Liz's picture of a society reporter. Rather, he seemed like an ordinary guy who might be more comfortable in McDonald's drive-thru than MacGregor's four-star restaurant downtown. She glanced down and realized his shoes hadn't been polished, then felt like a snob for even noticing such a thing.

Clearly, the society column must be a stepping stone for a young reporter like him. She should know better than to judge, seeing as she hated whenever anyone did it to her. And yet, how could she not form an opinion when his words and motions seemed to contradict one another?

Liz cleared her throat as Dorian placed his hand at the small of her back and began to guide her in a dance. She would be nice, at least for one dance. After all, it wasn't his fault her father had married Vanessa Price.

"So you write for the paper?" she asked conversationally. "What drew you to that?"

He smiled sharply, and she was taken aback by the suddenness of it, the forced nature of the gesture. His voice remained smooth, buttery. "Hey, I'll be the one asking the questions here."

She nodded. The sooner she gave him what he wanted, the sooner she would be free of him. "Okay. Shoot."

"It's a beautiful wedding," he said the moment Liz had granted permission. His words rolled over one another as if each was pulling the next along. "Ben Benjamin is your father. Is that right?"

Liz nodded.

"And your mother wasn't invited?" He hooked an eyebrow, waited. Both of which told Liz he already knew what her answer would be.

"My mother is dead."

"Oh, sorry." He frowned, but there was no sorrow in it. He'd known about her mother. What else did he know? And why had he bothered to learn these things about her?

She sighed and said what she was expected to whenever anyone brought up her mother. "It's okay. It happened a long time ago. I never really knew her."

Dorian's smile returned, completely at odds with his words. "How did she die?"

"She died while having me," Liz whispered. She didn't like talking about her mother with strangers. Mostly because she didn't have much to say once she revealed the cause of her death. Liz had never known her mom, and her dad didn't speak of her often. He would probably discuss her even less now that Vanessa was part of their lives.

"And that was... What? In 1990?" He knew, he knew exactly what he wanted to ask—knew the correct date, too. So why was he faking it?

Her warning bells chimed loud and long like a grandfather clock counting out the stroke of midnight. Their dance had only just begun. She'd hold out until the end of the song, then she would say goodbye to this pesky man once and for all. Until then, she'd play her part as expected, but she refused to give anything away. "'94, but I don't see what that has to do with the wedding."

"You're right. Sorry for prying." He chuckled as if her suspicion amused him, or perhaps it was her naïveté he found so endearing. Whatever the case, she didn't like him at all.

"It's okay," Liz said, even though it most definitely wasn't. "Just ask the questions you need to know for your column."

"Right, right." He paused as if the slight change in script had completely thrown him off his game. "There are a lot of mirrors," he commented, then pointed over to the nearest table as if somehow Liz hadn't already noticed this for herself.

She grabbed hold of this innocuous change in topic and decided to milk it for all it was worth. The more they could talk about harmless things like Vanessa's interior design preferences, the sooner the dance would end and she'd be free. "Vanessa loves mirrors. When she moved in, she brought at least half a dozen of them with her. She hung some where the walls were empty. Others, she put up in place of my dad's paintings and photos."

Dorian smirked, and she wondered if perhaps he didn't like Vanessa very much either. "Just your typical vain politician, huh?"

15

"That would be off the record, please. And again, off topic." Liz glared at him. If her words weren't keeping Dorian in line, perhaps a warning glance would do the trick.

He stumbled over his speech as he rushed to change the topic once again. "The, uh... The food was good. Did you have the salmon?"

"No, I'm allergic to seafood." Okay, so maybe he didn't know everything about her. Maybe the first couple of details had simply been lucky guesses.

Dorian didn't seem troubled or surprised by this information. "That's unfortunate for somebody living in Alaska. Tell me, have you lived here your whole life?"

Again with the questions that had nothing to do with the wedding. She couldn't tell what this man was trying to get at, and she didn't like this dizzying dance of cat and mouse. It was time to call him on how inappropriate this all was. "Yes, but why does that matter? Are you trying to interview me, flirt with me, or interrogate me? Because right now I really can't tell which it is."

"Flirt with you?" He laughed a deep, throaty sound. She hated it. Hated him. "No, no. You're really not my type. Sorry."

"Don't apologize to me. You aren't my type, either. Enough with the personal questions, okay? What more do you need to know for your article? How to spell names? Which flowers made up Vanessa's bouquet?" He seemed to know enough about her to believe that he was too good for her, and she knew enough about him to know that she didn't like him. Could this dance just end already?

He smiled as if delighting in her continued capture. "Sure, tell me that."

"The flowers are roses, peonies, and dahlias."

"Pretty flowers. Do they represent anything?"

"Yeah, love. I guess. Isn't that the point of this whole big thing?" She gestured around the room as best she could without bumping into other guests on the dance floor.

"You tell me." Dorian smirked at her, and she took a deep, steadying breath to keep from losing her cool. This exchange was growing more uncomfortable by the minute.

Liz shrugged and cast her eyes down toward Dorian's unpolished shoes. "I'm not really much of an expert on things like that."

"Yeah, that doesn't much surprise me. What are you an expert at? Painting? Music? Horseback riding?" His eyes locked onto hers as he listed each potential hobby and seemed to widen around the word "horseback."

Claims he's not flirting and then asks questions like that? Liz thought, her anger growing as she recalled the haughty laugh Dorian had unleashed at the mere suggestion that he might be flirting.

"That is oddly specific and wholly inappropriate. I trust you got what you need for your article?" Liz flung her hands away from his shoulders, and the rest of her body followed as she turned away from the dance floor.

Dorian followed, too, that same self-satisfied smirk filling out his face. "Oh, I got plenty."

"Good, then goodbye. I think this song is over anyway."

She felt his eyes on her as she marched toward the restroom. How long would she need to stay hidden to avoid answering any more awkward questions from Dorian Whitley? And why had the vision of a large chestnut horse with a white spot on its nose flashed through her mind when he'd asked her that last question?

Liz had never ridden a horse a day in her life.

Yet somehow the image seemed so real.

Almost like a memory.

Whatever spell Dorian had cast on her during their dance was clearly the work of dark magic. Hopefully he would write his stupid article and then disappear from her world for good.

CHAPTER 4

"Is he gone yet?" Liz asked her friends when she exited the bathroom about fifteen minutes later.

"He is," Scarlett confirmed. "But it was really weird..."

"Yeah, he kind of looked through your things first." Lauren frowned as she made this revelation.

"My things?" Liz searched the room, her heart racing. Her instincts were dead-on. This guy was definitely up to something, and a big part of her was afraid to find out what that might be.

Scarlett placed a hand on Liz's shoulder. Her voice came out soft and worried and not like Scarlett at all. "Yeah. Your pumps, purse, pashmina. All of that."

Liz contemplated telling her friends about their strange encounter on the dance floor, but she didn't want to worry them until she knew more. Besides, they had another problem to focus on right then. "I can't believe this. *What a creep!* Did he take anything?"

Lauren shrugged and shot Scarlett a worried glance. "Shane scared him off before he had too much time to root around, but you may want to check. Just to be sure."

Liz marched back to the table with her friends and, sure enough, her clutch had been left open when she was certain she had closed it. Nothing was missing. She made sure of that. But why? Why had this stranger taken such an interest in her? Why had he invaded her privacy so thoroughly? And why did she feel as if he were still here, watching her from the shadows?

"I saw you two arguing earlier," Scarlett said, her eyes widening. "What was *that* about?"

"Not arguing," Liz corrected. "But he was seriously over-stepping some boundaries. Like he had the right to question my entire life just because he's writing some puff piece on Vanessa. And then he insulted me."

"Insulted you?" Lauren grimaced. She'd always been fiercely protective of her friends, and she and Liz had bonded last year over their shared love for Lolly Winston's music.

"Yeah, when I called him out on being nosy, said he might be flirting. He laughed and said I wasn't his type." She tried to make light of it, but the rejection still hurt. Strange men who rifled through her things weren't Liz's type either, but still, nobody liked to be insulted. Especially on such a sensitive day already.

Scarlett's face grew as red as her name. "Well, he's not your type either!" she shouted.

Liz couldn't disagree there. Although Dorian had been tolerably handsome, his personality and decorum left too much to be desired. "It's almost like he knew something we didn't know, and he thought he was better than us because of it."

"Nobody—and I mean, *nobody*—is better than you, Lizzy," Scarlett said, wrapping her in a hug.

"Yeah, forget that jerk and let's go dance," Lauren said as she stretched her arms around the both of them.

"Shane and I will stay here in case he comes back," Henry offered after clearing his throat. "Go have fun, ladies."

Liz reached for her purse. Even though she trusted the guys, she'd still feel safer if she had her things with her.

Scarlett followed suit, grabbing up the pashmina and draping it over Liz's shoulders like a cape.

"I think I'll leave the shoes," Liz said with a laugh. "I'd actually be happy if someone decided to walk away with them."

"That bad?" Scarlett asked, shaking her head.

"That bad," Liz confirmed.

"What a passive aggressive monster," Scarlett said with a

sneer, grabbing Liz by the hand and tugging her toward the dance floor.

"Yeah, and there are, or were, at least two monsters here tonight, too." She shivered as they crossed over the spot where she and Dorian had shared their tense dance.

Scarlett lifted her arms overhead and bumped her hip into Liz's. "Enough with the monsters and witches. Let's dance."

Liz tried to lose herself in the music, but despite her general fitness, she had a hard time keeping up with her friends who regularly raced and ran sled dogs, making them the very definition of "in shape."

"It really is a shame," Lauren said after a while as the band prepared for their next song. "If you ask me, he was kind of cute."

Scarlett scrunched up her face in disgust. "*Ick*, Lauren. Really?"

Their friend just shrugged. "I mean, you never know, right? Sure, he's a creep now, but Shane wasn't exactly Prince Charming when we met the first time. Or second. Or, umm, third."

Liz laughed. She hadn't known Lauren back then, but she'd heard plenty of stories, each more amusing than the last. Still, Shane had turned out to be a prince in disguise. Dorian could only be a monster.

She sighed and tried not to show how much the

encounter still bothered her. "We may have danced at the ball, but Dorian is no prince, either. And I'm definitely not Cinderella."

"Cinderella would have been so much cooler if she had your red hair," Scarlett said, boinging one of Liz's curls that had fallen loose despite copious amounts of hairspray.

"It's really not fair, though," Lauren said. "Seeing as you got the evil stepmother, but not the prince. Fairytales are supposed to be more balanced than that."

"Fairytales?" Liz laughed. "I'm just trying to live a normal life here."

Just then, almost as if on cue, Liz's new stepmother, Vanessa, strode over to the group. Though she wore a practiced smile on her face, her body language suggested she was anything but happy.

And poor Liz seemed to be the object of her malcontent.

Vanessa grabbed her by the arm and pulled her in close as if to dance. Instead she squeezed her fingers hard around Liz's soft flesh and hissed in her ear, "Just what do you think you're doing?"

Liz gasped and tried to pull away, but Vanessa held tight. "Dancing with my friends."

"Who was that man, then? Don't think I don't recognize the press. They were not invited for a reason."

"He was writing a society piece and needed to know

about the flowers that were in your bouquet and other details like that."

Vanessa's grip loosened. "Are you sure?"

Liz nodded, though she wasn't sure at all.

The older woman let go, leaving little white and red marks on Liz's skin where she had squeezed. "For your sake, I hope no family secrets make their way into this weekend's papers."

Liz found it funny that Vanessa only considered her a member of the family when their reputation was at stake, but said nothing as she watched Vanessa make her way back across the hall. Every few feet, she stopped to greet another guest, giving hugs, smiles, and kisses on cheeks.

Of course the woman was kinder to near strangers than to Liz. If she loved her father so much, shouldn't she also love Liz? Or was that love missing for the both of them?

Liz couldn't make sense of it, no matter how hard she had tried.

She needed to put Dorian Whitley clear out of her mind, too. She had bigger, more immediate problems to worry about, after all.

CHAPTER 5

LIZ FINALLY HAD HER DRINK, BUT IT DIDN'T HELP THE WAY she had hoped. Throughout the evening, odd flashes lit up her mind. More than once, she thought she saw Dorian lurking in the far corner of the room, but every time she went to investigate, she found no one there.

She kept replaying their exchange, wondering why he would have asked the specific questions he did and why the mention of horseback riding had created such a vivid image in her mind's eye. She fell hopelessly short of any answers.

Luckily, her friends kept her occupied. That is until Lauren and Shane had to leave early to make the long drive back to their home in Puffin Ridge, and Henry and Scarlett decided to leave shortly after so that Henry could study for an upcoming exam for his med school program.

So Liz found herself alone, unprotected, vulnerable.

As the night pressed on, a few random guests asked her to dance. None, however, were so handsome or so infuriating as a certain Dorian Whitley. Still, she smiled, nodded, played the part. Appearances were of the utmost importance to Vanessa, which sadly meant they were important to Liz now, too. She'd gotten very good at pretending in the course of this one never-ending evening.

It wasn't until her father asked her for a dance that she finally let her unease known.

"You look beautiful tonight, sweetie," he said, swaying with her to the band's cover of "Butterfly Kisses," a song meant specifically for fathers and daughters.

"I don't feel it," she answered with a sigh.

His eyes searched hers, and she wished she could tell him everything without coming across spoiled or ungrateful. When he didn't find the answer in her gaze, her father asked, "Is something the matter?"

"It's just Vanessa. I don't think she likes me very much."

"Oh, Lizzy. That's not true. If anything, she likes you too well."

Liz scoffed. She couldn't help it. "Well, she has a funny way of showing it."

"You must understand where she's coming from. For more than twenty-five years, it's just been you and me against the world. It's intimidating to come into that. I think she feels as if she will always come second, and no new bride wants to feel that way on her wedding day."

"I guess..."

"She loves you because I love you. I know you two don't have the best track record, but she's trying, sweetie—and I know you are, too. That's all I want for us. To be a family." He pulled her close in a part hug, part dance. She felt his strong, steady heart, knew it had always beat for her. Now it was time to beat for someone else. It was all a part of growing up for her, moving on for him.

He squeezed her hand, and the edges of his eyes crinkled in a grin. He was a handsome man, her father. A good man. It was no wonder Vanessa Price had noticed. He took a slow, wistful breath and said, "Her girls never had that, you know. Their father left when they were both very young. Be good to them while we're away. I know Vanessa is very worried."

He tucked a stray auburn curl behind his daughter's ear and sighed. "Just like it's always been you and me, Lizzie, it's always been the three of them."

"And now it will be the four of you, and the one of me." Liz wished she could take the words back, but they were already out there.

Her father didn't look angry, sad, or shocked. He simply held her close and said, "You are always welcome back home, Lizzie. Always."

She loved him so very much, and she hoped Vanessa did, too. His new stepdaughters as well.

"Are you happy, Dad?" She had to know, and she knew he would never lie to her when asked directly.

He hummed to the music for a few beats before answering. "Of course I'm happy. I'm far happier than I deserve."

His answer made her want to cry. "How could you say that when you're the best person I know?"

Liz's father chuckled softly and pulled her in closer to his chest. "Well, you don't know too many people, but thank you. And for the record, you are still my favorite person in the world."

They used to say this to each other when Liz was small, and the exchange comforted her now, proved that even if Vanessa was determined to put a wedge between Liz and her father, he would always keep them close. She batted her eyelashes as she always had and asked, "In the whole wide world?"

"A million times around," he answered, pulling her hand up to give it a kiss.

Liz couldn't deny that her world was changing, but as long as she had the man who had always anchored it for her, she would be okay.

No meddling stepmothers or probing journalists could take away what they had. This would always be theirs.

CHAPTER 6

L<small>IZ CRIED AS SHE HUGGED HER FATHER FAREWELL</small>. H<small>E</small> <small>WOULD</small> only be gone for ten days, but somehow it felt like an eternity would pass without him. At least she would have this time to get to know her new stepsisters, seeing as she would be playing babysitter while their mother was away.

A sense of calmness took over her as she drove the three of them back to her childhood home, the place where they now lived instead of her. The wedding had come and gone. It was over. Time to move on.

Because that's what people did...

They moved on. Grew up. It had been well past time she moved out of her father's house and started making a life of her own. Her new sisters, Victoria and Valeria, were only fifteen and seventeen years old, each more than ten years her junior. They'd never known a father, much the same way she had never known a mother.

They deserved this second chance at a family, even if Vanessa Price didn't.

Liz's Akita, Samson, was overjoyed to be back at the big house. He made due in the two-bedroom apartment where she and Scarlett lived with both Samson and Scarlett's rescue Huskies, Fantine and Cosette, but things were more than a little cramped having two women and three high energy dogs in one small space.

She laughed as Samson ran up and down the stairs, then straight to the kitchen to beg for a treat from the fridge.

Valeria, who also stood in the kitchen, wrinkled her nose. "Why'd you bring him with you?"

"Because he's my dog. Where I go, he goes." Liz patted Samson's head and smiled to show him everything was okay despite Val's hostile tone.

The girl crossed her arms over her chest and sighed dramatically before saying, "Well, I'm allergic, so..."

"Are you sure?" Liz asked, doing her best to keep her voice even. Samson may not speak English, but he understood when he wasn't wanted. "I mean, your mom didn't mention anything about dog allergies, and it's too late to set him up at a kennel."

The elder of the two stepsisters, Victoria, entered the kitchen and traced a path toward the fridge, moving Samson with her foot so she had better access to grab a can of St. Croix. "Actually, I'm allergic, too." She sneezed, and Liz hoped for the girl's sake she didn't plan on auditioning for any plays. Acting was clearly not a strength of hers.

Victoria took a long, slow drink from her can, then fixed her eyes on poor Samson. "It's okay. I'm sure he wouldn't mind staying in the garage. It's only for a little over a week."

How about you stay in the garage and see how you like it? Liz thought, but she managed to stop herself from saying that aloud.

She waited for the girls to finish whatever they needed in the kitchen and head upstairs for the night, then she gathered the comforter from her bed and some old pillows and made Samson a bed in the garage.

His ears drooped as he realized that she would not be staying out with him.

"I'm so sorry, boy. It's only for the night. I'll bring you back in during the day, whether or not they're allergic, which—between you and me—I highly doubt. You know you're my good boy, but sometimes it's just easier to grin and bear it, you know? Besides, for whatever reason, these people make Dad happy. And we want Dad to be happy. Don't we, Samson?"

Samson swished his curled tail weakly against the ground and stayed in place as Liz stood and returned inside.

Tomorrow she would bring Samson back in after the

31

girls left for school. When they came home, she could point out that their allergies didn't seem to be acting up and tell them Samson would stay in the house for the rest of the week.

She was the one in charge, and she needed Samson's company to keep her strong and help speed the days along until her father returned to take her place.

Liz hoped Victoria and Valeria were nicer to him than they were to her, but somehow she doubted it.

It's only for ten days, she reminded herself. *Just ten.*

She tried to picture her father and Vanessa *en route* to their tropical honeymoon, laughing, smiling, enjoying each other's company. But instead she saw Dorian turning his nose up at her, invading her privacy, triggering her in every sense of the word.

Somehow she knew she would be seeing him again.

And when he turned up the next time, she would be the one asking the questions.

CHAPTER 7

On Monday morning, Liz had to drag Valeria out of bed kicking and screaming. Victoria was no help at all. She actually left for school without her sister, meaning Liz had to drive the tardy sophomore herself.

"I didn't sleep well because of my allergies," Val said without apology. It was enough to make Liz give up on not only her stepsisters, but quite possibly on ever having any children of her own, too.

All of this made her late for her job, but thankfully her manager didn't seem to mind.

"Rough night?" her boss, Sofia Stepanov, asked with a subtle quirk of her lips that was decidedly not a smile. Sofia often looked amused, but very rarely smiled.

"Rough morning more like," Liz answered with a sigh. "I

have never in my life been so happy to come to work for an opening shift."

"Keep talking like that and I just may have to give you a raise," Sofia said, heading toward the display window with new outfits for the mannequins. Her knee-length polka-dotted skirt swished as she walked with bold strides and a practiced swing to her hips.

Even though they worked at a trendy chain store, Liz was pretty sure her boss wouldn't be caught dead wearing the clothing—employee discount or no. Sofia was everything their store wasn't. She'd dyed her naturally blonde hair black with a slight tint of purple. Her snowy complexion was offset with flared eyeliner and a bright red lip, and though she was stylish in what she chose to wear, her outfits looked as if they belonged to a 1950's pinup model rather than a twenty-first century retail franchise manager.

Sofia caught Liz staring and offered one of her rare smiles. "Like it?"

"I'm sorry. My mind was somewhere else entirely," she answered, realizing then that while she'd been looking at Sofia, she'd been thinking of that creep, Dorian.

"You sure you don't need a sick day or something?"

Liz shook her head. "I'm not sick."

"A mental health day?"

"C'mon," Liz said, finally smiling herself. "We both know

if the company allowed mental health days you'd never even bother to show up for work."

"*Hardy har har,*" Sofia shot back sarcastically. "Hey, did I show you my new tattoo?"

"No, and I don't want to see it if it's not somewhere decent." Liz rushed to cover her eyes. Sofia was known for flashing her backside to any who asked to see the first of her twelve tattoos, a crescent moon that rose over her right butt cheek.

"Relax, it's just on my shoulder." Sofia undid the top two buttons on her dress and slid the sleeve down to show a patch of reddened skin and a new watercolor tattoo - an apple with a snake wrapped around it.

"Uhh, it's nice, I guess." Liz would never tarnish her skin like that. Besides, she couldn't think of a single thing she loved enough to emblazon upon her body forever. And with needles, too. Yup, no thank you.

Sofia gave her a devilish look, even though they both knew she was one of the nicest people in all of Alaska. "The forbidden fruit," she explained, pointing to her chest. "Because things are always more fun when you aren't supposed to have them. People, too."

"Whatever you say, Sofia." Sometimes Liz wondered if they would be friends were it not for work. While she liked Sofia's individuality and brazen disregard for other people's opinions, Liz had to confess that the two of them were as different as any two people could come.

"You know I'm right," her manager answered with a wink, buttoning her shirt back up. "Now tell me about your weekend, Miss Manners."

Liz told her about the wedding, the missing place setting on the stage, even the weird interrogation on the dance floor from Dorian. Somehow it felt safer confiding these things in Sofia rather than in Scarlett or Lauren. Besides, if push came to shove, her manager would always have her back—and Liz didn't doubt the woman knew how to get the best of just about anybody in a fight.

"I would have slapped that woman," Sofia declared. "That would really give the reporter guy something to write about. *Society*." She rolled her eyes. "What are we living in, the eighteenth century?"

"Well, you're not wrong about that point," Liz said as she carried some new stock from the back room and began to parse some of their older pieces for the clearance rack. "And I wish I could give Vanessa a piece of my mind, but it would hurt my dad too much."

Sofia tsked. For as tough as she seemed on the outside, Liz knew very well she kept her heart in a carefully concealed box, locked away deep inside her chest. "You're a saint. And what about those girls and their allergies? They are totally faking it!"

"Again, you're right. But what can I do?" Liz wished she could have called Sofia in to handle all her problems these past twenty-four hours, but more than that, she wished she was strong enough to handle them herself.

"I don't know, but you have to do something. You can't just let people take advantage of you, because they're mean enough to try. Sometimes life can be a battle. And you need to arm yourself for it. You know?"

Who hurt you, Sofia? Liz wanted to ask, but she knew better than to question her boss. Besides, she admired her too much to talk down to her, even if it was out of a desire to help.

Liz shrugged. "Actually, I don't. I've never exactly had these kinds of problems before."

"Oh, honey, you are a lucky one then." Another flash of a smile.

What would Sofia do? Liz wondered. When faced with Vanessa, Valeria, Victoria? Dorian? *WWSD?*

She wished she knew herself well enough to think about what she would do, what she should have done. But sometimes it felt like Liz knew everyone else in the world better than she understood her own heart.

Sofia Stepanov was easy to understand, but what of Liz Benjamin?

Someday soon, she hoped to figure it out.

CHAPTER 8

MONDAY MORNINGS WERE ALWAYS SLOW AT THE SHOP, which gave Liz and Sofia lots of time to catch up. Around noon, Sofia headed off toward the food court where she liked to people watch during her lunch break. This left Liz to sweep the floors and do some extra tidying up in the hopes they would see a busier afternoon.

She hummed along to the radio as she cleaned, not realizing someone else had entered the store until a shadow fell over her path. She turned quickly and saw none other than Dorian Whitley with his hand raised as if he were about to caress her from behind.

"You!" she spat with a cold, hard voice she barely recognized as her own.

"*You.*" He gave this rejoinder without blinking, then added, "I didn't know *you* worked here."

Liz didn't believe this visit was anything other than pre-meditated. She wanted to call Dorian out on it, to yell until he went away, but she knew better than to chew out a customer in the middle of the sales floor. Even if Sofia didn't care, the franchise owner would. And Liz would be out of a job faster than she could bat an eyelash.

"Well, now you know." She sniffed and turned away. While she doubted her stepsisters were allergic to Samson, it definitely seemed she'd developed an aversion to Dorian Whitley.

"Wait." He took quick steps, coming up in front of her again. "I need your help."

She laughed in his face. "My help? You mean with your article?"

He shook his head, keeping his expression blank. "No. With finding an outfit."

"An outfit?" Liz asked, raising a hand to her hip. She doubted he could afford to shop here given the crumpled, tired look of his current outfit, but it was her job to help anyone willing to spend money at her store. "What do you need the outfit for?"

"For meeting my girlfriend's parents," he said smoothly. Dorian proved to be a much better liar than her stepsisters, but somehow, she knew he wasn't being honest with her.

She stared straight into his dappled green eyes, but they gave nothing away. "Your girlfriend?"

"Right. Like I said before, you're *not* my type. My girl-friend is much prettier than you. Her name is Janie." His eyes widened as if he expected this revelation to make her feel something. She honestly still didn't know whether he was flirting or interrogating—and she couldn't be sure which option she preferred, either.

Liz rolled her eyes and groaned. "Are you ever nice?"

He smiled, and it almost made him seem charming. "Not if I can help it."

"Well, unfortunately, I have to help you. Which I'm guessing you know, and that's why you're here. But I refuse to talk about anything other than which clothes you should get."

Another smile. This one so wide it showed off two rows of perfectly white teeth. "Whatever you say."

"Good. Now, tell me where you're meeting Janie's parents, so we can pick an outfit and get you out of my store." Liz didn't have any friends named Jane—let alone Janie—yet the name did seemed familiar. She wondered if perhaps she had met Dorian's girlfriend once upon a time. That is, if such a mythical being could even exist in the real world.

As it was, she trusted nothing that came out of Dorian's mouth.

"We're going horseback riding and then having a picnic on the beach," he explained.

Liz sighed. Again with the horseback riding. He had mentioned it during their wedding dance, asked if she was a fan. Her mind again flashed to the brown and cream animal looking out from beneath long, dark lashes.

"Well, that sounds like a nice evening. You should stick with jeans for the outdoorsy stuff." Liz led Dorian over to the wall display filled with jeans of all washes, sizes, and styles. "You look like a 34 tall. Go with the dark wash. It'll hide the dirt better. Here." She grabbed a pair from one of the higher shelves and pushed it into his chest. "Try these on."

"Actually, these are way out of my budget." Not a hint of embarrassment flickered between them. Either he was incredibly used to being poor, or he had come for a reason other than shopping.

Liz would hardly be surprised by either possibility. "The clearance section is in the back," she muttered, doubting he would bother to keep up the charade.

She traced her way back to the register and waited behind the counter until Dorian left the store. She didn't have to wait long, because about five minutes later, he returned with a frown on his face.

"Yeah, I'm not going to get anything, but thanks anyway," he said, hovering near the counter.

"Okay, buh-bye then." She gave a sarcastic little wave, hoping he'd just leave already.

41

But Dorian looked as if he wanted to say something more. He licked his lips, and...

The return of Sofia saved Liz from having to hear whatever he had planned to say. She walked straight up to Dorian with the fake smile she'd perfected for their customers. "Hey, there. Welcome to our store. How can I help?"

"He was on his way out," Liz answered for him, staring at him, daring him to say otherwise.

Sofia shrugged and disappeared into the back.

Liz watched her walk away, and by the time she turned back toward Dorian, the store was once again empty.

Did Dorian get what he came for, or would she be seeing him again before whatever this was had been finished?

His visit did accomplish one thing. Liz spent the rest of the day fuming, wishing she had never met Dorian Whitley.

A part of her felt as if she still hadn't met him.

This man had secrets—perhaps about her—and she'd only come face to face with his false front.

Next time, she wouldn't be so polite. Next time, she would expose the true man beneath the mask.

Scars and all.

CHAPTER 9

LIZ VOLUNTEERED TO CLOSE UP SHOP THAT NIGHT SO ONE OF the high schoolers who worked evenings could leave early for a date. Sofia offered to stay back with her in case that "creepy guy shows up again," but Liz waved her off, knowing her manager used her few hours off each night to design and sew her own fashion line.

She loved Sofia's passion for clothing. It reminded her of Scarlett's dual passions for both books and dog sledding. Liz had never pursued anything quite so intentionally, but she often found herself happy—no matter what she ended up doing to pass the time.

That is, until Vanessa Price stormed into her perfect little life, leaving a trail of wreckage and a pair of evil stepsisters in her wake. Like Liz, her friend Lauren had been directionless in life before moving to Alaska and falling in love with both the Iditarod and one of its most infamous mushers.

Lauren had lacked passion, though she had always craved it. Liz didn't need much to be happy. She simply preferred a steady, stable life. Something it seemed she might not have anymore.

As she locked up shop for the night, she felt an odd chill wrack through her body. When she glanced around the dark parking lot, she saw no one. Just her mind playing tricks on her.

Again.

Still, she pushed down on the locks the moment she was seated safely in her car and drove home faster than she should have. She needed a nice cuddle with Samson, a good night's sleep, and no stepsister drama to get her through the rest of this day.

But when she pulled up to her father's house, she found that this plan was not to be.

Beat up cars and pickup trucks were wedged along every inch of curb for at least two blocks in either direction. Some had even pulled haphazardly onto the lawn and, sure enough... music was blaring at maximum volume from somewhere within the bowels of the house.

She checked the time on her dashboard clock. It was only a quarter past eight, yet it seemed that this party had been going on for hours. And on a Monday night, too!

She was going to kill Victoria or Valeria. Okay, both. She'd kill both now and ask questions later.

But then Vanessa would probably kill her. Way too much bloodshed for what was supposed to be a quiet Monday night at home.

Liz got out of her car and slammed the door shut. Even though she was mere inches away from the sound, it hardly reached her ears. The heavy bass and thumping rhythm of the party music was so heavy, it almost felt as if the ground beneath her was shaking.

Maybe it was.

If the police hadn't already been called, they would be soon. Liz just hoped she wouldn't be deemed responsible for whatever had gone on inside during her absence.

She stomped toward the front door and flung it open, seething with rage. She wasn't even thirty, and yet somehow she found herself playing the part of the wet blanket parent ruining a random group of teenagers' fun.

A few kids near the door glanced over at her, but then quickly turned their attention back toward each other and whatever liquid their plastic cups contained.

Liz didn't want to know. *Couldn't* know.

She scanned the room for Victoria or Valeria, but instead she found the very coworker whose shift she had agreed to cover that evening. That explained how the girls knew she would be out long enough for them to host a party. They were so grounded, and Liz would never, *ever* cover a shift for a high schooler again.

This needed to stop, and it needed to stop now.

"That's enough!" she yelled, placing her hands around her mouth to form a megaphone. "Party's over!"

Nobody heard her, or maybe it was just that nobody cared.

She groaned and then flicked the light switch on and off, which only excited the dancers more. Apparently, she still looked too close in age to the high school partiers to be taken as a serious threat to their fun. Ending this thing was not going to be easy.

A hand spread across the small of her back, startling her. Was someone seriously putting the moves on her? *Ick.*

She spun around, ready to give the inappropriate Romeo a piece of her mind, but the man who greeted her wasn't a teenager at all.

It was Dorian Whitley.

CHAPTER 10

"You!" Liz's blood boiled at the sight of Dorian in her house. If this were a romantic comedy, she might say something like "fancy meeting you here" or "we have to stop meeting like this." But this wasn't a comedy. Ever since the appearance of Dorian, her life had become a tragic drama—and she definitely didn't remember buying a ticket.

Dorian smiled without a trace of his normal bluster. "Me."

Again with the flirting-not-flirting-interrogation-not-interrogation. She had enough to deal with already and hated him for adding to the unwieldy pile up of problems. She placed her hands on her hips and glowered at him. "You're following me, and I'm calling the police."

He waved his phone at eye level. "I already did."

Well, that was unexpected. "But, you... You..." Liz struggled to find words to match the situation. She'd vowed to give him a piece of her mind should they meet again. Yet now that he was here and the party music was thumping at her brain like a bass drum, she came up short.

He placed a hand on her back again. "C'mon, let me help you break this up. Then you can decide whether you want to have me arrested for stalking."

His touch felt nice, comforting, given the horror of the situation. The pleasantness of it angered her greatly. "So you admit it?" she spat.

He nodded and smiled. This time, she believed the gesture. He'd smiled many times during her past two encounters with him, but this was the first one that felt authentic. "I do, but I have a very good reason."

"Well, will you tell me?"

"After we handle this. Where's your dog?"

"Samson, he... How do you know I have a dog?"

"I promise to explain everything. Just tell me where Samson is."

"The garage, probably."

"Perfect."

Liz stood rooted to the spot as Dorian pushed through the house and toward the garage. He knew exactly where to go, which unsettled her to no end. Had he been in her house before? Why? Why did he know so much about her? Why had he followed her home? And why did he suddenly want to help her?

A moment later, Samson burst into the kitchen through the garage and began jumping excitedly on various party guests.

A girl shrieked when Samson's leaping caused her to spill her drink all over her top.

"Party's over!" Dorian shouted when everyone's eyes turned toward the kitchen. "You have two minutes before I start ordering my dog to attack, and probably about three before the police show up."

Victoria stomped over to Liz, her face twisted with rage. "You're ruining my party!"

Liz wanted to be nice. She wanted to keep it together for her father's sake, but she'd had enough. "You shouldn't be having a party! It's a Monday night, and nobody here is old enough to be drinking."

Tori rolled her eyes as if Liz were the ridiculous one in this situation. "My mother doesn't like you, and neither do I."

If that was meant to surprise Liz, it didn't. It just annoyed her further. "Yeah, and right now I don't like you very much, either." She pushed Tori out of her way, but the girl charged after her.

"Your boyfriend is ugly!" she shouted.

"And you're grounded," Liz shouted back. Teenagers

sucked, especially *these* teenagers. Liz, for her part, had never been so happy to be a grown up in all of her life.

Victoria stomped back away, trying to keep her guests from leaving as she threw herself into dancing to the loud pop music playing over the speakers.

Dorian came up behind her, as was starting to become a particular habit of his. "Ugly, huh?" He laughed but didn't wait for Liz to defend him. Despite his brief willingness to help her clear out the party, he'd done nothing to earn her trust—or her favor.

And Liz had many things she could have said to that. That his face wasn't nearly as ugly as his personality. That actually she found him to be quite handsome when he wasn't insulting her.

Instead, she just shook her head.

"Look, I didn't really call the police," he admitted. "I didn't want to get you in trouble."

"Who are you? Why won't you leave me alone?"

"I'm Dorian Whitley, reporter for *Anchorage Daily News*."

"That's what you said before, but I don't believe you."

"Well, it's the truth."

"Then why did you follow me to work and follow me home? Why do you know about my dog and know your way around my father's house? What else do you know that you're not telling me? And aren't you supposed to be out horseback riding with your girlfriend's parents?"

He shook his head and gave her a look she couldn't decode. "I don't have a girlfriend."

"So that part was a lie."

He placed his hand on her back again. It seemed almost possessive this time and far too intense given the nature of their relationship. "A convenient bending of the truth."

Liz needed everyone out of her house and she needed them out now, including—and especially—Dorian Whitley. "Look, if you didn't call the police, then I'm going to. Even if I get in trouble for the underage drinking, it's better than being left alone with a lying psycho stalker."

"Ouch. Tell me what you really think of me." He seemed amused more than hurt, but the insult had clearly scratched beneath the surface. *Finally.*

"I just did. Now, will you leave on your own, or do you need to be forcibly removed?"

"Don't you want the truth?"

"I don't think I trust you to give it to me."

"Look, it's complicated. I—"

Now she waved her phone at him. "You have five seconds."

"I lied about having a girlfriend, but my name *is* Dorian and I *am* a reporter."

She scowled at him and pressed a button on her phone. "*9,*" she said aloud as a warning.

"I'm not stalking you. I'm working on a story. Just like I told you at the wedding."

She pressed another button. One more to go and she'd have the police on the line. "*1.*"

"The story isn't about the wedding. It's about a political scandal with Vanessa."

That caught Liz off guard. Her finger hovered over the last button, but she didn't press down. Not yet.

"Your father may be in danger. *You* may be in danger."

"Are you for real? Do you actually expect me to believe that?"

"From what I know of you so far, I doubt you will. But it's the truth."

"So what do you want? Why are you following *me?*"

"Access. You don't like me, but I'm pretty sure you like her even less." He let his words hang between them, waiting for her response. Liz finally understood the expression about the rock and the hard place. Should she go with Dorian, who claimed to be the enemy of her enemy and thus her friend, or should she go with the woman who her father loved and, to her knowledge, hadn't stalked Liz a day in her life?

Decisions, decisions.

CHAPTER 11

LIZ WATCHED AS SOMETHING CHANGED IN DORIAN. HIS expression softened, and his lips twitched in amusement. Even his eyes, which had once seemed so cold and hard, beheld her now with concern, perhaps even kindness. Was this the same man who took such delight in insulting her? That seemed hard to believe.

And yet...

She searched the room for any sign of her stepsisters, but they had both disappeared into the rush of departing partiers outside. A few more teens staggered from the kitchen, the bathrooms, and upstairs, and then Liz was alone with Dorian.

"Okay, so what? You want me to help bring her down?" she asked, her voice low, unsure.

What she lacked in confidence, he covered doubly. His eyes flashed a pair of excited emeralds as he said, "Precisely."

Liz had known in her gut that Vanessa Price was up to something sinister. Hearing Dorian confirm it only made her worry about her father more. As if knowing she needed the extra help to come to grips with the one-eighty change in their relationship, Dorian reached for her hand and gave it a reassuring squeeze.

From enemies to allies—could it really be? Though her skin warmed at his touch, she still had a hard time trusting him—and for very good reason. He'd insulted her, investigated her, stalked her. None of those were winning tactics when it came to making friends.

But whatever the case, he seemed to know something she did not. Something important.

"Why do you say we're not safe?" Liz asked with a shaky voice.

Dorian grabbed her hand again, then took the other as well. Liz felt a charge run up her arms, but didn't have enough wherewithal to figure out whether it was anger, fear, or... something else.

"Because you're not," Dorian insisted. "Vanessa has done some very unsavory things and has made a lot of people angry. It's only a matter of time before it catches up to her."

"My best friend, Scarlett, is one of them. Vanessa tricked

her out of a job last year. Scar is okay now. She loves her new life, but it was really hard."

Dorian nodded emphatically. "Yes, I believe it. And to think Scarlett is one of many, *many* people Vanessa Price has hurt. She's not even the worst of her victims, either."

Liz dropped his hands. They were distracting her from the more important topic at hand. She knew Vanessa had evil in her, but there was still one very important thing she couldn't figure out. "I still don't understand how we could be in danger," she whispered, feeling a chill run over her as she did.

He continued to smile lightly, though his words were intense. "I know it's asking a lot, but you'll just have to trust me until I can reveal more."

"It *is* asking a lot. You lied about your article before. How do I know you're not lying now?"

"You don't," he said plainly. "But I'll keep investigating whether or not you allow it."

She crossed her arms and turned away, muttering over her shoulder, "So I may as well invite you to stalk me?"

He placed a hand on her shoulder and whispered, "It's not stalking if I have permission, and actually now that you're willing to talk to me, I don't need to invent reasons anymore."

His breath caressed her skin and sent a fresh shudder through her. It seemed her body was every bit as sure of its reaction to Dorian Whitley as her brain wasn't. "So that's why you made up a girlfriend?" she whispered with her face turned away.

He spun around her, bringing them face to face. "Yes."

"And the horseback riding?"

Dorian's eyes widened before he looked away and cleared his throat. "It's just something I thought you might enjoy. I thought we could use it to build a rapport with each other."

"I've never ridden a horse in my life, which makes me doubt your investigative skills or your honesty." She had every reason not to trust him, and only one to try.

He smiled, his serpent like charm returning. "Which is it?"

She shook her head and frowned, not wanting to encourage him when she still didn't know whether his sins could be overlooked in order to form a partnership. "Take your pick."

"You don't have to know everything yet. You just have to know enough to allow me some access to the house, to Vanessa's life."

She wanted to trust him. She did. Because if he were telling the truth and she ignored it now, it could mean very real pain for her father down the line. But she needed to know, "Will you ever tell me the full truth?"

Dorian looked away as if to regroup, then turned the full

intensity of his gaze back her way. His furrowed brow seemed to hint that he felt frustrated either with her or with himself. "We're very close to blowing the lid off this scandal," he said rather than directly answering her question.

"And then?"

"And then your part in this is done." He still wasn't giving her any promises, but she needed him to make at least one that night.

"What about my father?" Liz demanded.

Dorian shrugged, but tension remained in his posture. "What about him?"

"Could this hurt him? This big thing about Vanessa? He is her husband, after all."

He studied her before replying. "You really love him, don't you?"

"Of course I love him. He's my father."

"He's been good to you?"

"What kind of question is that?"

He placed a hand on his chest reflexively. "One from the heart."

"Yeah, my father is a good man. Don't hurt him with this, whatever it is."

"I will do my absolute best."

"Promise?"

He didn't blink as he answered, "You have my word."

"Okay, then what do you need from me?"

"Show me to Vanessa's office. Give me some time to dig around, find the evidence I need." His anxiety seemed to dispel completely. She'd given him what he wanted, but would that be enough?

She needed to know where all this was heading. "And then?" Liz asked again.

"And then I'll leave quietly. You can forget you ever met me if that's what you want."

"Fine. Just don't let my stepsisters see you."

He chuckled now. "Oh, I can be very stealthy."

The way he said this made Liz wonder if he'd been following her longer than she knew. If he'd already known her intimately before ever introducing himself at the wedding.

And, even more unsettling, whether he was the only one.

CHAPTER 12

DORIAN LEFT ABOUT A HALF AN HOUR LATER, SAYING HE HAD what he needed but not offering much more than that. Samson had an upset stomach from lapping up spilled beer and vomited freely into a pair of one of the stepsisters' sneakers.

And Liz felt too tired to care anymore. At least he was getting it out of his system and serving up a bit of much needed karma.

"Good dog," she told Samson, then plopped down onto the couch with an afghan and a mug of tea.

She grabbed her phone and sent a text to Scarlett: *Ugh. Is it next Monday yet?*

Scarlett's reply came back almost instantly. *That bad, huh?*

Worse.

The phone buzzed again, but this time with an incoming call.

"Talk to me. What's up?" Scarlett said.

"*Everything*. Everything's up." She told her friend about the party, the fight with her stepsisters, and even about Dorian.

"Can I come stay the night with you?" Scarlett asked when Liz had finished weaving her tale of woe.

"What for?"

"Seems like you could use a friend."

"But what about Fantine and Cosette?"

"I'll ask our new neighbor, Celeste, to keep an eye on them for tonight. Don't need those sisters of yours creating any more trouble about their—*cough, cough*—allergies."

"*Step*sisters," Liz corrected with a sigh. "That first syllable is important."

Twenty minutes later, Scarlett was seated beside Liz on the sofa. She'd worn her favorite flannel pajamas, ready for their grownup sleepover and leading Liz to wonder if she'd gone from being dependent on her father to being dependent now on her roommate. Whatever the case, at least she didn't have to face the rest of the night alone.

And she felt especially happy to spend it with her best friend.

She and Scarlett had always been close, but Liz hadn't realized how important their friendship was to her until

Scarlett all but disappeared in pursuit of her sled racing dream, and for nearly a year.

Thankfully, their friendship had only grown stronger and Scarlett had gotten a fairytale-like ending—scoring both a dream guy and the ultimate adventure in the process. Yup, Scarlett kind of had it all, but she'd also lost almost everything to get it. Liz was proud of her friend's resilience and inspired by it.

"How's your novel coming along?" Liz asked as she sipped at her second mug of tea that night.

"Great! I even have a couple of agents who have contacted me through my blog, asking to see the manuscript when it's done. But you know? I think I might want to self-publish."

"Self-publish? Why?" Liz liked to read, but had no idea how the publishing world worked. She'd always thought writers ended up self-publishing as a last resort for books that no one else wanted.

"Well..." Scarlett took a sip of her tea, too. "These days, most authors do better with self-publishing, but money's not really an issue for me."

"Of course it's not with that rich fiancé of yours," Liz teased, even though Henry had chosen to forego his family fortune and make his own way as a doctor.

"The thing I like," Scarlett said thoughtfully, "is the control. I can get my books out there faster, and I won't have to deal with anyone changing parts of the story that are important to me."

Liz nodded along. "That makes sense. How soon will your book be done?"

"It's hard to say, because this is my first novel, but it's really getting there. Maybe by the end of the year it will be ready to grow its wings and fly into the hands of my millions of adoring fans."

"Millions, huh?" Liz chuckled. "Well, I know I'll be buying my copy."

"You better buy two!" Scarlett teased, making a silly face that was all Scar-Scar.

Sometimes her best friend seemed larger than life. At least, larger than *Liz's* life. Scarlett marched to her own beat, whereas Liz tended to strut about to whatever song was already playing.

"And you really don't miss it?" Liz asked after a few moments of companionable silence. "The thrill of the race, I mean."

"Well, seeing as I almost died the one time I ran the Iditarod, I think I'll be okay reporting from the sidelines. I still get to be a part of it, so yeah. I'm happy." Scarlett smiled to show she meant these words with all she had. Liz hadn't discovered a single passion, yet her best friend was blessed with two. Not only that, but she'd found a way to make both a major part of her life.

Liz wondered if she'd ever find that for herself.

A loud thumping sounded on the stairs, and a few moments later, Valeria stood across the room. It was amazing at how loud a one-hundred-and-twenty pound girl could be when she wanted to prove a point.

"It wasn't my party, you know," Val said, crossing her arms over her chest and staring accusatorily at Liz. "It was all Tori's idea, so I don't think I should get in trouble over it."

Liz wanted to tell Valeria that she no longer cared what either of the sisters did, but she knew her father was counting on her to keep them safe while he and Vanessa were away. She shrugged, hoping it came across casual. "I saw you with that drink in your hand, so don't act all innocent with me. You're grounded, too."

"But that's not fair!" Valeria stomped her foot like a fuming bull.

"Not fair, huh?" Liz forced a laugh. "Would you like me to call your mother to get her opinion?"

The girl narrowed her eyes and said between clenched teeth, "You'll never be our sister, and your dad will never be our dad."

That was enough to send Scarlett spiraling into action. "Drama queen much?" she asked, jumping to her feet in defense of both Liz and the father she loved like her own.

"*Whatever*," Val retorted. "I never asked for our parents

to get married, and I definitely never asked to live in a house with you and your smelly dog."

Everyone looked over at Samson, who lay quietly by the fireplace. The girls hadn't discovered his vomit puddles yet, but at least he seemed to be feeling better now. At the sight of so many eyes on him, the dog dropped down into play position and broofed hopefully.

Val groaned. "*Ugh*. He's even more clueless than you are!"

Samson came over and happily buried his nose in Val's crotch. She grunted and knocked him away with her knee.

"She didn't ask for this, either, you know," Scarlett interjected. "And I'm pretty sure she likes being related to you even less than you like being related to her. And you better treat Mr. Benjamin nicely. At least now you have one decent parent."

"What's that supposed to mean?" Valeria hissed.

Scarlett laughed bitterly. "Do I really need to tell you what a shark your mother is? Okay, let's see. We've got—"

"Scar-Scar, stop." Liz put a hand on her friend's wrist and pulled her back onto the couch.

Scarlett fell back onto the cushions with a defeated plop, and Valeria seemed to delight in the fact she was the last one standing.

"Well, now you have two things to put on your shopping list for tomorrow, Lizzy," she said coldly. "A leash for your dog and a muzzle for your friend." With that, she spun on her heel and ambled back up the stairs. A moment later, the door to her bedroom slammed shut.

"I honestly don't know who's worse," Scarlett mumbled while playing with a loose thread on her pajama pants. "The apple or the tree."

"Just wait until you meet the other apple. She's even worse."

"Impossible!"

"It would seem that way, but yeah, she's actually that bad. They all are."

"My poor Lizzie," Scarlett said, wrapping her friend in a hug. "Promise me one thing?"

"What's that?"

"If that Dorian guy turns up again, let me help, too. He may be creepy, but he's nowhere near as bad as that trio. Deal?"

Liz clinked her mug against Scarlett's, though their tea had long since grown cold. With Scarlett on her side, anything felt possible now.

CHAPTER 13

L IZ LEFT WORK EARLY THE NEXT SEVERAL DAYS TO AVOID A repeat of Monday's party fiasco. Sofia understood and granted her the time off, but Liz's pocketbook definitely was not pleased. Now that she had rent to budget for, she needed all the shifts she could take and dollars she could earn.

Still, problems aside, the week was almost over.

Soon her father and Vanessa would be back from their honeymoon, and she would be back home in the apartment she shared with Scarlett. It was funny how quickly the apartment had become home and how quickly the house she'd lived in her entire life had begun to feel like it belonged to somebody else.

Hopefully, once his newly-wedded bliss wore off, her father would find a way to spend time with Liz separate from his new family.

As for the current week from hell, it all ended after one last weekend spent playing punishment warden to Victoria and Valeria. Maybe they could actually try to do something fun together on Sunday to top the week off with a beautiful cherry of a memory.

She sincerely doubted it, but that didn't mean she couldn't at least try.

She *would* try.

That Friday afternoon, Liz arrived back at the house before either of the girls. Checking the clock over the stove, she realized they both should have been back at least fifteen minutes ago.

Okay, maybe there was weekend traffic or some kind of after-school club that they attended and Liz didn't know about. She'd feel better, though, if she could confirm with her stepsisters via text.

On your way home? She typed, then waited for the read receipt and reply. She had never seen either Tori or Val without a phone attached to their hands, so she expected the reply to come quickly.

But no response came until the front door flung itself open about ten minutes later.

"*Ick*, that sucked." Valeria scowled, dropping her backpack by the door and heading toward the stairs.

"What's wrong? Where's your sister?"

"*What's wrong is* I had to take the bus, because my sister

decided to play hooky after lunch and never came back to get me."

Panic flooded Liz's chest. Here she'd thought things couldn't get worse than the party, only to find they could get far, far worse than she'd ever imagined. "What? Tori wasn't at school this afternoon?"

"That's what I just said." Val rolled her eyes. "Now can I please go?"

"Not until you tell me where she went." As rude as she was to Liz ninety-nine percent of the time, at least Val did what she was told. For that, Liz was thankful now.

Her stepsister shifted her weight from foot to foot, eager to be free of the conversation. "I don't know. It's not like she invited me."

"Can you text her for me? Ask when she'll be back?"

Valeria grunted. "Why can't you?"

"I already did, and she's not answering."

"Fine." Val's fingers moved quickly over her phone. "There. Now may I *please* go to my room?"

"Okay, but let me know if you hear anything from Tori."

Val raised her hand and made the okay sign, then disappeared into her room. A moment later, music swelled from her stereo, the missing sister apparently forgotten.

Liz checked her phone again. Still no read receipt from Victoria. Where could she have gone, and why was she still out? She had to know that Liz would tell her parents, and no matter how much Liz disliked the girls' mother, she knew Vanessa wouldn't let her daughters get away without a punishment.

And, more than likely, a severe one.

She called Scarlett, Lauren, and Sofia to tell them what was going on and to get their advice.

"She'll turn up soon enough," Sofia said dismissively.

"Want me to call around for you?" Lauren offered. "Or, if I start driving now, I could be there by six at the latest." Bless her heart, she wanted to find a way to help despite living more than two hours away.

Scarlett answered Liz's call with a groan. "*Ugh*, I would help you search, but I'm stuck at this lecture thingy. It's my first time writing for this one blog, and… totally horrible timing. I'm so sorry! But, hey, let me know if you still haven't found her later tonight, and I'll come over and help with the hunt."

An hour passed, two.

Still no sign of Tori.

Liz asked Val to text again, but the girl still hadn't heard anything regarding her sister's whereabouts and appeared to be a bit worried herself now.

Liz wracked her brain as to where Tori could have gone. The truth was, she knew next to nothing about either of her stepsisters. She could search the places she'd hung out during her high school years, but Victoria was very different than she had been growing up.

Liz was studious and well-behaved, whereas Tori wasn't just the life of the party—she *was* the party. Val offered a few suggestions as to where Liz could check and even offered to come with her, but Liz insisted she stay at home in case Tori returned.

Should Liz call her father and Vanessa? She hated to spoil their honeymoon when they only had a few days left, but at the same time, wouldn't they want to know?

She couldn't decide, and she'd run out of people to call.

Except...

"What's up?" Dorian answered on the first ring, and relief washed over her. She still didn't trust him, but she knew he was good at figuring things out. Maybe he could figure out where Victoria had disappeared to and help bring her home safely.

At least he had been true to his word and hadn't shown up in her life unannounced since their talk on Monday. That had to count for something, and even if it didn't, she needed the help.

"My sister is missing. Tori, the one who threw the party. She's not answering her phone, and I'm kind of freaking out."

"I'll be right there," Dorian said before hanging up.

Liz paced the living room as she waited for him to arrive, realizing she hadn't even needed to ask for his help.

He'd offered it all on his own.

CHAPTER 14

LIZ JUMPED INTO DORIAN'S TRUCK THE MOMENT HE PULLED into the driveway. She hadn't expected some James Bond-esque vehicle, but she was still surprised to find that such an old rustbucket had gone unnoticed while following her about town.

"When did you last see her?" Dorian asked as he pulled out onto the main street.

"In the morning. Before school." She placed a hand on the dashboard to steady herself from the uneven ride.

"And you have no idea where she might have gone?"

Liz shook her head, tears ready to spill. Victoria had been missing for hours now. It had been her job to protect her stepsister, and she'd failed spectacularly.

"No idea at all?" he asked again, his mouth set in a firm line as he waited for her response.

"No, I wish I—" Her response was cut off by a wracking sob. It wasn't like Liz to cry, but it also wasn't like her to lose a teenager—or to team up with her stalker.

Dorian yanked the truck hard to the left. The sudden change in direction threw Liz up against him, but he offered no apology or explanation.

"What's going on? Do you know something?" she asked in disbelief.

"I might," he said as he pushed down hard on the gas pedal, jolting the old truck forward at an impossibly fast speed.

"I don't understand. How could you...?"

Dorian glanced her way, and she could see it then. All the fear, the worry. This man wasn't her enemy. Perhaps he'd never been. "Let's focus on bringing your sister home," he said.

"Why are you helping me?" Liz stared at Dorian as they spoke, but he kept his eyes glued straight ahead.

"I wish I could tell you."

"But you can't?"

His entire face changed in that moment. The usual cock-sure grin had been replaced by a look of melancholy. And not just melancholy, but what appeared to be genuine fear. "Not yet."

"Not ever?" She had to know what was going on, and it seemed Dorian was the only person who had the answers.

73

"I don't know." He frowned, but looked like he wanted to say more—like he wanted to say everything.

"What is it?" she prompted. "Please talk to me. You're the only lead I have right now on finding Tori. I'm terrified and need to feel like I have someone in my corner."

He turned to her with a beseeching glance before turning his eyes back to the road. "Listen, if my instincts are right on this, you're going to learn some pretty unsavory things about me. You probably won't like me very much when you do, but please try to give me the benefit of the doubt."

"I already don't like you very much."

He sighed. "Yeah, I deserved that."

"But I do appreciate you helping me now." She reached out to touch his hand on the steering wheel. It was the most comfort she could offer in that moment, but somehow, she knew he needed it. He tensed, then softened beneath her touch.

"Just try to remember I'm not all bad." The truck jerked to a stop outside a hotel downtown. "We're here now. Get out."

Liz's heart dropped to the floor. She left it behind in the cab as she stepped down onto the sidewalk with shaky feet.

Dorian seemed frightened, too, which only scared her more. "I hope we're not too late," he said through gritted teeth.

Liz tried to match his pace as he ran right through the lobby and up the stairs. This was a man who knew exactly where he was going. But how?

They exited on the fourth floor.

"Stay in the hall," Dorian instructed, using his body to shield the door.

"What? No!"

"Please trust me on this, okay?" He wouldn't look at her, and he wouldn't back down.

"But what if she—? Oh, God. What if she…?"

"She won't be," he answered with a shake of his head. Liz could tell she was wearing on him, but she refused to be sidelined.

"How could you possibly know that? How did you know to come here? Talk to me, Dorian." Liz hated being told what to do when it came to Tori's safety. That was her responsibility, and she needed to be the one to set things right.

"Do you want to stand here talking, or do you want me to save Victoria?" He turned toward her suddenly, and the intensity of the green in his eyes startled her.

Liz gulped down her protests and waited as Dorian burst into the room, shoulder first. She hadn't even seen him pull out a keycard.

"Ahh, Dorian." An older male voice with the slightest

Southern accent floated out from the room, quickly followed by a young female voice she knew very well.

"You're interrupting my shoot!" Tori protested.

Liz didn't need to hear anymore. She pushed through the doorway and past Dorian.

"Well, who's this then?" the man asked with a chuckle. His well-groomed salt and pepper beard was the first thing she noticed. The second were his hands. They were rough and weathered, in stark contrast to his polished outfit and hairstyle. Who was this man? "Could it be the infamous Janie?"

Liz marched right up to her sister and grabbed her by the arm. "I'm Tori's sister, and I've come to take her home."

Victoria did not appreciate this. "But Lizzy! Mr. Warwick was taking my pictures for his modeling agency. I'm going to be a star!"

"The hell you are. Let's go," Liz hissed, absolutely refusing to back down or to let go. "*Now*."

"Sorry, my dear. I must have had you confused with someone else." Mr. Warwick chuckled, approaching her slowly and taking her hand before she could think to pull it away. "Liz, was it?"

Dorian pushed Liz back toward the hall, then grabbed Tori by the wrist and forced her out of the room, too.

"Hey!" Tori whined. "Your boyfriend is ruining my rise to stardom."

"I told you to stay in the hall," Dorian growled.

"Who was that man?" Liz demanded.

Dorian turned to her with hollow eyes. "Trouble."

CHAPTER 15

"That was really embarrassing," Tori pouted, arms crossed over her chest, as Dorian drove them both back home.

"Don't even get me started," Liz said. She couldn't even look at her stepsister then, nor could she look at Dorian, which meant her eyes remained focused outside. "What were you doing alone in a hotel room with a man who was more than old enough to be your father? And you cut school to do it, too. What were you thinking?"

"It's not a big deal, Liz. Don't worry about it." Liz could hear the eyeroll in the girl's voice. Did she really not understand the gravity of this situation?

"How could I not worry? Tori, he could have..." She dropped her voice to a throaty whisper. Just thinking of what could have happened made Liz want to cry all over again. "He could have taken advantage of you."

Tori refused to budge in her anger. "But he didn't, okay? He was trying to help me, and now that you made that huge, big scene, I doubt he will."

"Good," Dorian said from the driver's seat, joining the conversation for the first time since they left the hotel.

"I don't like you," Victoria said with a scowl.

"I don't care," he shot back, not taking his eyes off the road. "How did the two of you meet? Tell me everything you can."

Liz wanted to tell Dorian to butt out of it. She wanted to demand answers as to how he could have possibly known where to find Tori, but she needed time alone with him first. Since she also wanted to know how Tori had hooked up with Mr. Warwick, she swallowed back her protests for now.

"He discovered me at the gas station, of all places," Tori declared proudly. "Said I had the exact look *Vogue* needed these days and that he'd help me put my portfolio together."

"And you believed him?" Liz asked, aghast.

"It's not like he asked for any money. And I told him I'd meet him after lunch because I had an English test second hour. Can you at least focus on the positive?"

The positive? That Tori had made one good decision and many bad ones? Liz had made some pretty dumb mistakes during her own teenage years, but nothing even came close to comparing to this. Was Tori really so clueless to the dangers of what she had done, or was she purposely holding back? Liz decided to ask her forthright. "And he didn't try to touch you, or...?"

"*Eww*, no."

Well, that was one concern abated, but there were still many left to address.

They arrived back at the house, and Tori slinked out of the truck.

"You're grounded!" Liz shouted after her through the open window. "*Again*," she added, realizing she'd already grounded the girls for their party on Monday night. "You are super, extra, mega deluxe grounded!"

"That was bad," Dorian said, studying his hands as they clenched and unclenched the steering wheel.

"I was so scared," Liz admitted, choking on the words as they came out.

"Me too." He reached for her hand.

But that was when she remembered everything that had come before safely delivering Tori home and ripped it away. "You! You knew exactly where to find her. You're responsible for this!"

"*No.* I never wanted this to happen." Dorian's hand shook as he tried to reach for hers again, but she refused to show him any kindness until she had some answers.

She looked up into his face, which had grown sickly white. "This was never about Vanessa, was it?"

And it grew whiter still as he answered, "No."

It was easier to fight with him when he appeared strong and healthy, but she felt so much anger toward him that his obvious remorse did little to dampen it. "Why is everything that comes out of your mouth a lie?" she demanded.

"Liz, I'm trying to help you. I'm trying to keep you safe. You shouldn't have come into the room. I—"

"So this is all my fault now?"

He took a deep, steadying breath, and some color returned to his cheeks. "No, will you just listen to me?"

"Why? So you can tell me more lies?"

"I don't *want* to lie to you, Liz." He reached for her hand again, and this time, she let him take it. If the gesture comforted him enough to help get the answers out, then she would tolerate it for now.

"Then tell me the truth for once," she begged. "What is going on?"

His face fell, and he squeezed her hand. "I wish... I wish I could tell you."

"You can't tell me? Even now?"

He nodded then shook his head in rapid succession as if warring with himself over how to answer. "It's not my place."

"Really? Is that *really* the reason?" If he was conflicted, then it was only a matter of finding the correct words to shift the scales in her favor. She tried to count to ten under her breath, but the next thing out of Dorian's mouth brought all her rage bubbling back to the surface again.

"And I signed a Non-Disclosure Agreement."

"Who the heck cares about some stupid NDA? Are you not understanding that my sister could have been raped or abducted?" She narrowed her eyes at him, squeezed his hand impossibly hard, forced him to recognize the seriousness of the situation. Her desperation.

"He wouldn't have done that." He shook his head adamantly. This time he was sure of his answer, but none of it told her why. Why had this man targeted her family? Why was Dorian a part of it?

"Who is this man? How do you know him?"

Dorian sighed, seeming more frustrated with himself than with Liz. "Charles Warwick, and we met only recently, but it didn't take me long to figure out that the guy's bad news."

"And what does he want with my sister?"

"Nothing. He's just using her to..." Dorian's words broke away, and he shifted his gaze to the seat between them.

"To what?" She willed him to look at her, but he wouldn't. Perhaps he couldn't in that moment.

"Look, I've said too much already."

"You haven't said anything at all!"

"Please keep an eye on your sisters," he mumbled, still unwilling to look at her. "Watch your back. Be careful."

"So we're all in danger, and that's the best you've got?"

He let go of her hand at last, looking genuinely grieved as he said, "It's all I can give you for now."

"Of course. Of course it is."

"Liz, you don't understand. I promise I'll—"

"No, no more of you or your promises." She unbuckled her seatbelt and hovered over the door handle. It was clear she'd be getting no more answers tonight. She needed time to think of a different strategy, to find some way to ensure her family would be safe. With time, would Dorian come around to helping them?

As she looked back at him one last time, she only felt doubt, distance. This was a weak man, one who was afraid of Warwick. If he couldn't fight for himself, how could he possibly fight for her? No, he'd already done enough as far as she was concerned.

"Goodbye, Dorian," she said as she walked away.

CHAPTER 16

THE WEEKEND WAS NOT OFF TO A GREAT START, AND LIZ had a feeling it would only get worse after forty-eight more hours confined in close quarters with her angry stepsisters.

She called the teenaged coworker who'd tricked her into the set up for Monday's party and demanded she cover her Saturday shift at the store. At least with high schoolers you could always threaten to tell their parents as a way of getting them in line.

This particular tactic, however, didn't work on Victoria.

"I can't wait until your mother hears all about the week we've had," Liz said when Tori had refused to do her assigned chores for the week.

"And I can't wait to tell her how you ruined my chances at a modeling career," the girl shot back.

Valeria either felt sorry for Liz or afraid of Tori, because

84

she joined Liz on Saturday to watch a cheesy romantic comedy on Netflix.

"*Classic,*" Val said around a mouth full of popcorn as the hunky hero declared his undying love to the heroine. When the credits rolled, she turned to Liz with a far-off look in her eyes. "Is that what it's really like?"

"What?" Liz asked as she tried to study the credits reel to find the name of the actress she couldn't quite place.

"You know," the girl said shyly, a tint of blush rising to her cheeks. "Falling in love."

Liz laughed. "I'll tell you when I know."

"But what about your boyfriend? The one that helped find Tori yesterday?" Val watched Liz as if waiting for some fount of wisdom. When it came to this matter, though, Liz's fountain wasn't just dry—it had never been filled.

Still, she couldn't let this certain misconception stand. "*Not* my boyfriend. For that matter, not even my friend."

Val shrugged. "He's cute, though."

Liz had to bite her tongue to stop herself from saying, "Yeah, if you like the creepy, lying stalker type." Because the truth was, she *had* noticed Dorian's good looks—and somehow, that only made her like him less.

Val reached for another handful of popcorn. "Do you think that guy wants to make Victoria a model?"

Liz bit her tongue again. As much as she worried they hadn't seen the last of Mr. Warwick, she didn't need to confide these worries in a fifteen year old. "I guess we'll see on that one," she answered noncommittally.

The doorbell rang, and Liz glanced over at the clock. Just a bit after eight. Not especially late for a Saturday night, but still...

"I'll get it!" Val volunteered, skipping toward the door. And then a moment later shouted, "It's some guy here to see you!"

Dorian.

He just needed to leave her alone already. She stomped to the foyer ready to give him a piece of her mind—no more biting her tongue that night.

But the man who waited for her on the stoop wasn't the one she'd expected to find. Dorian would have been a welcome guest compared to...

"Mr. Warwick," Liz said coldly. "Could you give us a moment, Val?"

Valeria left after some hesitation, but Liz had a feeling she'd stayed close to listen in from a nearby room.

Liz stepped out onto the porch and shut the front door behind her. Immediately, the cold night air gave rise to goose flesh on her arms.

"What are you doing here?" she asked the man.

He didn't answer right away. Instead, he looked at her with eyes so wet, she expected tears to fall at any moment.

The broken man before her today was very changed from the one she'd met just yesterday. "Liz?"

"Yes. What do you want?" She folded her arms over her chest, not liking the way he was looking her up and down. His eyes didn't linger on her body, but she still felt vulnerable under his gaze.

"I'm sorry about yesterday. It was the only way I could think of to..." His voice fell away and the tears rushed down his face, getting lost within his beard.

Tears or no, she refused to feel sorry for this man. He'd already proven his character, as far as she was concerned, and the jury had not decided in his favor. "I don't care what your excuse is. Stay away from my sister."

"*Step*sister," he corrected with a sad smile.

"That doesn't matter. I don't know what your game is here, but you shouldn't be preying on young girls. If I see you anywhere near her again, I'll call the cops."

He shook his head, a smile edging to the corners of his mouth. "I wouldn't do that if I were you."

"Is that a threat?" She bristled from his sudden change in demeanor.

"No, it's just..." His smile grew even wider. "It's not me they'd arrest."

"You're not making any sense." She took a step back, and her heel caught the edge of the door frame.

Warwick closed the gap between them with one large step forward. "Don't you remember me?"

"I've never seen you a day in my life." He was too close. She was too vulnerable in this position. She needed him to leave. Now.

"No, of course you haven't, *Liz*." He spat her name out like it was poison. His sudden shift in emotions startled her. She felt far more afraid standing here with Warwick than she ever had with Dorian.

"You need to go now, please." She tried to sound strong, but there was no mistaking the quaver in her voice.

He didn't back down. Instead, he placed his hand on the edge of the house, mere inches away from her face. "Let me come in to talk. Let me explain."

"I told you to leave." She hoped the words came out braver than she felt.

When Warwick still didn't turn to leave, she decided to be the one to do the leaving. Reaching behind her for the doorknob, she attempted to slip back inside the house.

But his strong hand grabbed the door before she could shut it behind her. "You need to talk to me. I came all this way."

"I don't need to do anything except call the police. Get out. *Now*."

But he pried the door open and followed her into the house.

Liz searched frantically for Valeria, but she was nowhere to be found. That left her alone with this strange man that refused to take no for an answer. If she ran upstairs, he would follow her and possibly threaten her sisters.

But if she stayed here...

She whispered a prayer: "Please, God. Help me."

Then hurled herself at the intruder with all her might.

CHAPTER 17

"STOP STRUGGLING," WARWICK GRUNTED, ATTEMPTING IN vain to block Liz's flurry of punches. He caught her by the arm before her fist could connect with his jaw, then whipped her around into a prisoner's hold. "I just want to talk."

"No!" she screamed, desperately trying to break free.

"Let her go!" Victoria cried as she and her sister charged down the stairs to Liz's rescue. And then they were upon the intruder, too. Together, the three of them kicked, punched, and bit, but still the man did not run away, nor did he fight back.

"Get out of my house!" a voice boomed from the doorway.

Everyone froze and turned their eyes toward Liz's father and Vanessa, who weren't expected to return from their honeymoon for another two days.

"You don't deserve this house. This life. None of this is yours!" Warwick hissed, turning toward Ben as if ready to uncoil the full force of the attack he'd been holding back.

"C'mon, girls," Vanessa said, ushering for her daughters to join her. "You, too, Liz," she added as she placed a hand on Liz's back and guided her toward the staircase.

"No, don't go!" Warwick tried to grab Liz as she passed.

"Don't touch my daughter!" Ben yelled, shoving Warwick hard.

"C'mon," Vanessa pleaded. "Let your father handle this."

Liz looked back toward her father, who nodded, and followed her stepmom upstairs.

The four of them took refuge in the master bedroom, and Victoria immediately burst into tears. "I am so sorry, Liz. This is all my fault."

"What do you mean, sweetie?" Vanessa asked, wiping the tears from her daughter's cheeks.

"I cut school and went with him to..."

"Stop, Tori. It wasn't your fault," Liz said as she paced back and forth across the room. "Something else is going on."

"We'll talk about all this later, okay?" Vanessa said before giving her daughter a big hug.

"What do you know?" Liz asked, turning toward her stepmother. "What does that man want? How does my dad know him?"

Vanessa shook her head. "I don't know. Someone called us at the resort, insisted on talking to your father, told him we had to come back early, that it wasn't safe. We were supposed to go scuba-diving tomorrow, but your father... he panicked, and—"

"Who called and why?" This was getting them nowhere fast. She wished she could just go back downstairs and talk with her father and Warwick, but the truth was, she felt frightened. She needed answers, but not at the expense of her safety... or even her life.

"I don't know." Vanessa frowned and shook her head. "I don't know the answers to either of those questions."

"Dorian," Liz said with a scowl. Who else could it be?

Vanessa perked up at that. "The reporter for the paper?"

"Yes. I mean, maybe. I'm not really sure who he is."

"But if he hadn't called when he did... I hate to think about what could have happened." Vanessa rose and pulled Liz into a hug, startling the both of them. "You mean so much to your father. I'd hate for anything to ever happen to you."

Her dad entered the room then. His mouth bled freely and his shirt was torn, but otherwise, he looked okay.

Liz flew into his arms.

"He's gone," her father said before any of them can ask.

"We need to call the police," Vanessa said, rifling

through her purse in her search of her cell phone. "Maybe they can still catch him."

Liz's dad walked over to his wife and nudged her hands away from her bag. "No," he said.

"What do you mean no?" Vanessa said with a nervous laugh. "He tried to hurt the girls. He *did* hurt you." She reached up to caress his face and sighed. "You're bleeding, Ben."

"Come help me get cleaned up, then."

"But the police...?"

His face was grave and left no room for argument. "No. I took care of it."

Liz fell back onto the bed after the others left to tend her father's wounds. Whatever had happened, she highly doubted it had been taken care of. Warwick's anger only grew once her father had arrived on the scene. This was a man who'd been willing to abduct a minor and force himself into her home uninvited.

Liz knew she hadn't seen the last of Warwick.

But the next time he turned up, she'd be ready.

CHAPTER 18

LIZ STAYED THE NIGHT AND HAD BREAKFAST WITH THE family the next morning. Vanessa served up eggs and bacon while gushing about their "marvelous" honeymoon.

"It really helped, the getting away," she said, adding another strip of bacon to each of her daughters' plates. "It was the perfect way to close out the old chapter of our lives and open up a new one."

Liz sighed. The old chapter didn't seem closed at all, at least not for her and her father. If anything, Dorian and Warwick had brought them a book they'd never intended reading yet still knew intimately.

"More bacon, sweetie?" Vanessa asked, turning her way.

"What I'd prefer..." Liz grumbled, "are more *answers*. Heck, any answers."

"Liz..." her father warned.

"I've got this, dear," Vanessa said, setting the fry pan back on the stove and then taking a seat at the table. She turned toward Liz. "Sometimes no answer is the best answer you can hope for."

Liz huffed. She couldn't believe what she was hearing.

"You don't see Tori and Val demanding an explanation, do you?"

Her stepsisters looked up at her briefly, than back toward their plates.

"The fact of the matter is, we all make mistakes from time to time. And we shouldn't have to live with them forever, should we?"

Liz's father began to rise from his chair. "Vanessa, I—"

His wife raised her hand, cutting him off midsentence. "It's okay, Ben. Let me take care of this."

She turned to Liz once more and took on a syrupy sweet tone. "The point is, sometimes we just need to move on with our day."

Liz glanced at her father, who was nodding adamantly. "Dad? Why won't you tell me what's going on?"

He cleared his throat. "Vanessa is right. We just need to do our best to move on."

"But he broke into our house. He—"

"Enough," he said firmly.

Liz pushed her chair back. She needed to get out of there before she exploded with rage. Her father had never kept things from her before. *Never.* And for him to confide in Vanessa instead of her stung deeply.

"If you won't give me the answers, I'll find someone who will." She grabbed another piece of bacon and popped it in her mouth before turning on heel and stalking out of the room.

She expected her father to follow her out of the kitchen, to at last agree to talk. But this new version of the man she'd always known inside out shocked her once more by simply letting her go.

Less than ten minutes later, Liz had packed up her belongings, and she and Samson were on their way back home to the apartment.

Their two Husky roommates, Fantine and Cosette, greeted them at the door with excited howls and lots of licks.

Samson dropped to his elbows and broofed, inviting his friends to take part in a wrestling match. The dogs yipped and growled and made such a ruckus with their joy that it woke Scarlett, who had still been in bed when they arrived. Liz often wondered how her sleepy friend had managed to wake up at the crack of dawn for nearly a year as she was training for the Iditarod.

"Liz?" Scarlett asked around a yawn. "Is it Tuesday already?"

Liz laughed. It felt so good to be home. "No, sleepyhead. My dad and Vanessa came back early."

"Okay." She yawned again. "What time is it? Is there more time to sleep?"

"Like, ten?" Liz guessed, but when they looked toward the microwave clock, they found it was actually closer to eleven.

Scarlett's eyes popped wide open and she raced back down the hall. "Shoot, shoot, shoot!" she cried.

"What's going on?" Liz smiled. Scarlett drama she could take all day long. It felt like a nice reprieve from the past week. It felt like coming home.

"I'm supposed to meet Henry. There's a race today, and we were going to go cheer our friends on." Her roommate raced up and down the apartment before returning to the kitchen with her toothbrush in one hand and a tube of paste in the other. As she readied her brush, she said, "Hey, since you're back, want to come?"

Liz wondered if her father planned to attend due to his unexpected early return home. She just wasn't ready to face him yet. Not until she knew more about what was going on and why he was hiding what he knew.

"Sure," Liz said with a laugh. "I could use a change of scenery."

"And you want to spend time with me before I head to Texas for a week, right?" Scarlett asked after spitting a huge wad of paste into the sink.

"*Ugh*, I forgot about that. Do you have to go?" Liz hated

the thought of staying alone in the apartment. Sure, she'd have the dogs, but would they be enough to keep Warwick away if he decided to pay her a visit?

Scarlett patted her on the shoulder as she passed by on her way toward her bedroom. "'Fraid so, but don't worry, I'll be back before you know it."

Oh, how Liz hoped she was right. Because it was beginning to feel as if everyone in her life was systematically abandoning her when she needed them the most.

CHAPTER 19

Liz and Scarlett arrived at Tozier Track about a half an hour later. Henry was already there waiting near the parking lot.

Scarlett ran at him full force and jumped into his arms, showering him with kisses. A stray reporter snapped a couple pictures of the pair that had once been known as "the star-crossed rivals." Most everyone had moved on, but articles about Scarlett and Henry still popped up on fan blogs every so often.

"Hi, Liz," Henry mumbled, setting Scarlett back down onto her feet.

She gave him a quick hug. It was funny to think of how vehemently she'd hated him just over a year ago. Back then, everyone had thought Henry took after his wicked grandfather, Henry Mitchell Sr. Only Scarlett had been willing to give him a chance—to see something more.

"Been here long?" she asked.

Henry shrugged. "Twenty minutes or so. The first racers should be coming in soon."

"Who's favored to win?" Scarlett asked, putting on her game face. Although she'd chosen not to race anymore, she still loved the sport with everything she had.

"Dallas, I think. But I know never to bet against a Ramsey."

"That's right!" Scarlett said proudly. During her year of racing, she'd stayed with Shane and Lauren Ramsey, cementing their already rock solid friendship.

"Is Lauren running today?" Liz asked.

"I think so," Henry answered. "But they may have..."

Henry continued to speak, but Liz no longer heard his words. It was as if all the sound had been sucked from the scene. Her heart pounded in her ears as Dorian stepped out from his truck and onto the gravel lot below.

"Hey, it's that guy from the wedding!" Henry said, breaking the silence. "The one who was going through your purse."

"I can explain." Dorian approached with his hands out in front of him. Even though Henry had proven himself to be kind-hearted many times over, people still tended to act cautiously around him. And Liz felt far safer having him here today.

"Can you?" Liz asked with an emboldened laugh. She was so sick of people stringing her along, lying to her, acting as if she didn't deserve to know the truth about her own life. "Can you really?"

"C'mon, babe. Let's give them some time to talk." Scarlett tugged on her fiancé's arm and led him over to the finish line. She didn't know the full story—heck, Liz didn't either—but Liz had filled her in on some of the finer points during their drive over.

Dorian stood at her side as they both watched Liz's friends walk away into the gathering crowd. "I heard about what happened last night," he said when they were fully alone.

Liz felt all the rage of yesterday build up in her once again. "You mean that Warwick broke into my house? That he tried to hurt me? That he did hurt my dad?"

Dorian frowned and looked away. "He wouldn't hurt you."

"How can you say that? You weren't there." Why had Dorian come if he still planned on being evasive? Would he finally work up the courage to tell her something more? She doubted it. Doubted *him*.

"Trust me. He wouldn't hurt you."

"Every time you tell me to trust you, it makes me suspect

you more. Why are you here?" She had no time for games or false assurances. What had happened last night scared her more than she cared to even admit to herself. She needed answers, or she needed to move on.

Dorian, however, had something else in mind. "To apologize."

Liz waited. An apology wouldn't be the worst thing in the world.

He sighed. "I'm so sorry I got you into this mess, that I led him to you." Well, that was unexpected.

Liz widened her eyes as if doing so would help her see better, help her to understand better, too. "You... you're working with Warwick?"

"Was. I quit last Wednesday." Dorian kicked at the gravel in the lot. Why was he avoiding her gaze again?

"But that was before the hotel with Victoria," she said softly.

"I know." He looked up at her for a moment, then back toward the track.

Liz moved into his line of sight, hoping a kind face would shake out the words he was struggling to hold back. "What happened on Wednesday?"

"Look, I can't tell you everything, but I need to tell you enough to keep you safe." His voice came out slow, hurried, almost like a whisper.

Liz almost couldn't believe what she'd heard. If she got him to admit one thing, she could get him to tell her more. But one serious problem remained. She didn't trust him and didn't know if she ever could. She crossed her arms and shook her head. "How do I know what's true and what's a lie?"

"Can we start over?" His emerald eyes looked so full of hope, as if they could forget the terrible ways their lives had intersected this past week and a half.

"If that's what it takes." She waited as he took a few deep breaths, cleared his throat, worked up the nerve.

"My name is Dorian Whitley. I'm a reporter for the *Anchorage Daily News.* It doesn't pay very well, so sometimes I take side gigs."

Liz shivered, inherently knowing he was about to make a major revelation. "What kind of side gigs?"

"I find people. I found you."

Now things were starting to make sense, but she needed more. "For Warwick? But why?"

"It's not my place to say."

"I need to know, Dorian. Please tell me."

He hesitated before grabbing each of her hands and holding them in his. "I want you to know, but I can't be the one to tell you."

"Because of the NDA?" She hated that he'd considered that stupid piece of paper more important than her family's safety, especially considering what had transpired on Saturday night. If he'd just told her…

"No, because it will hurt you," he whispered, almost afraid to speak the words aloud.

"You said Warwick wouldn't hurt me," she reminded him.

"I don't think he will, but the secret that brought him here…" Dorian bit his lip, cutting off the rest of the sentence she so desperately wanted to hear.

"Why are you trying to protect me? You don't even like me."

"That's not true," he said emphatically. "I tried so hard not to, but everything about you, Liz. You're my perfect girl."

Another unexpected twist. In less than two weeks, Dorian had gone from arrogant reporter to psycho stalker to unexpected friend to… a romantic suitor? This was absurd. Even more absurd was the fact that she didn't hate the idea. Not just because she could use his feelings to find out more, but also because he did genuinely seem to care. He seemed closer to helping her find the answers to her problems than even her own father. "You said I wasn't your type."

"Because you're the subject of an investigation. It's not ethical. I could—"

"You were mean to me. You stalked me. You insulted me every chance you got."

"I didn't know what kind of man Warwick was until… When I found out, I started following you to keep you safe. In case he…"

Liz couldn't handle this. Dorian's revelations only heightened the tension between them. She needed him to stay focused, to do whatever it was he came here to do. "Please finish a sentence already!" She hadn't meant to sound cruel, but her tolerance was quickly falling away like sand in an hourglass.

Dorian fixed his gaze on her once more, hardly blinking as he said, "Liz, I told him he got it wrong. Told him you weren't the one he was looking for. I tried to alter the DNA reports before he could see them. I—"

"DNA! How did you get my DNA?"

"From your hairbrush. The night of the party. I tried at the wedding, but couldn't get a good sample."

"I can't believe this." Another confession. Another terrible invasion of privacy. What more was he hiding? How much crazier could this thing get? This was not Liz's world. Not her life. She wanted things to go back to the way they had been, but knew that would never happen now. For all the awful things Dorian had already revealed, he was holding back the worst truths in an attempt to protect her.

He blinked hard, frowned. "You don't have to believe it, but it's the truth."

"You say you like me, but you led a psycho straight to me. You stole my DNA. What else have you done?"

"Nothing else, I swear. And with Warwick, I thought I was helping you. I didn't know..."

"Okay, so say I believe everything you've said so far. You're still leaving out the most important piece of information. Who is Warwick, and why did he hire you to find me?"

"I can't tell you. It's not my place."

He'd already told her far more than she knew that morning. If only she could find a way to learn more. "But—"

"I'm sorry!" he called, jogging back to his truck and leaving her behind. "Please don't hate me."

Liz shivered. She felt many things in that moment, but hate was not one of them. Could she change Dorian's mind?

CHAPTER 20

"PLEASE DON'T GO! I NEED TO KNOW WHY!" LIZ FELT AS IF her knees would buckle beneath her as she watched Dorian climb into his truck. All the revelations—and especially partial revelations—swirled around in her brain, threatening to knock her off balance.

Dorian had been hired by Warwick to find her.

He had stolen her DNA, and the test seemed to confirm whatever answer the two of them had been searching for.

Dorian stopped working for Warwick when he realized how dangerous the man could be. This same man had attacked both her and her father the previous night.

Now Dorian was trying to protect her. Said he had developed feelings for her against his better judgment.

But he wouldn't tell her why.

She still didn't know everything.

She knew the effects, but what she really craved was the cause. Who was she to Warwick? How did his father know the man? Why did he refuse to call the police?

None of it made sense.

Liz's world had always been ordered, logical. Happy, quiet. But all that had changed the day Dorian Whitley entered her life.

A sudden spring breeze blew past, and Liz gasped from the cold.

Dorian turned to look back at her one more time before disappearing into his truck. He was leaving, but there was still so much more she needed to know.

She wanted to run after him, but her legs wouldn't budge. So instead, she stood in the center of the parking lot, watching, waiting, hoping he'd return—and this time, with the full truth.

And then another gust, a blonde tornado came tearing by. Scarlett, whose hair did not match her name, ran right past Liz and bolted behind Dorian's truck before he could finish pulling out of his space.

Liz watched as she beat his rear window and said, "Hey, you owe my friend some answers! Get back out here!"

Henry came up behind Liz and put a steadying arm around her.

She turned to him and asked, "How much did she hear?"

"We came back to check on you, make sure everything

was okay. We saw him leaving and you shaking and crying, asking for him to come back." She tried to focus on Henry's eyes—one blue and one brown—to feel some safety and comfort in their familiarity, but all she could think about was Dorian, that he had almost left her here, alone, confused, crying.

"Is that all?" she asked with a sniff.

"That was all it took to send Scarlett into protective mama bear mode. Are you going to be okay?" He frowned and hugged her into his side. It seemed Henry had a bit of bear in him, too. Did that make Liz Goldilocks, a hapless intruder that had to be tolerated, or else avoided? It sure felt that way lately.

"I honestly don't know," she said with a long, shaky exhale.

"Sounds like the story of my life, too. It will be all right, though. Scarlett and I will make sure of it."

Liz tried to smile, but Henry had no idea just how big the mess he was promising to fix had already become.

Scarlett marched back over to them, pushing Dorian along with her almost as if he were a prisoner. In a way, perhaps, he was. "Now get talking," she demanded of him.

Dorian faltered. "I... This is really between me and Liz."

"And the guy that attacked her last night." Scarlett's expression was fierce, unforgiving. It was no small wonder she had survived her plunge into an icy lake despite the overwhelming odds against her survival. "You wouldn't tell her, so now you have to tell the three of us. *Now talk.*"

Dorian's voice was strained, hoarse even. "Liz, please. Don't you understand? I'm trying to protect you."

"What makes you think she's not capable of protecting herself?"

Dorian turned toward Scarlett. "You have no idea what she's up against. *I do.*"

"Then tell me. Tell us. I mean, if that's okay with Liz?" Scarlett glanced her way, and Liz nodded. She had been unable to get the answers from Dorian on her own, but perhaps Scarlett's more direct approach would get her the information she needed.

"Ja—" Dorian coughed and shook his head. "*Liz*, please listen to me. I like you too much to upend your entire world like this. What I know will change everything about your life, and I don't think it will be for the better."

"Likely story!" Scarlett said with a bitter laugh. "You'll say anything to take the heat off yourself, won't you? I have half a mind to—"

"Scar, stop." Henry spoke gently, but his words were firm. It was then that Liz realized she still stood with his arm around her, protecting her from the rest of the world. "He's telling the truth."

"How could you possibly think that? This guy is as shady as they come, and he hasn't told the truth yet. That's why we're all here." Scarlett eyed Dorian wearily and placed her hands on her hips.

Henry squeezed Liz tight, then let her ago, approaching his fiancée as he spoke. "Don't you remember where we were less than two years ago? I had to live a lie, day in and day out, and it ate me up. That's why I wanted you to know the truth, because you meant something to me."

Scarlett softened, but still held onto Dorian's arms to prevent him from getting away. "And I had a hard time believing you."

"I don't see how this is the same," Liz said, finally joining the conversation. "Henry had never done anything wrong. Everyone only assumed he had. But Dorian admits to leading Warwick right to me. He admits to stalking me and stealing my DNA."

"Really?" Henry asked. "You did all that?" Maybe he already regretted trying to defend the other man, but no one seemed to regret Dorian's choices more than he did himself.

Dorian nodded sadly. "But I didn't know her, and I didn't know how crazed my employer would become. You have to believe me when I say I thought I was helping."

"But you didn't help," Scarlett pointed out. "You made everything worse."

"Yes." Dorian shifted his weight from foot to foot as if ready to flee. "But I'm trying to fix it now."

Liz had regained some strength and was ready to jump

back into the fight—if fighting was what it would take to finally win her battle against all the secrets and lies. "How? How can you fix a problem you won't even identify?"

"I already told you. It's not my place. Talk to your father, then give me a call." Dorian turned to leave once more, and Scarlett was quick on his heels to prevent his escape.

"Stop!" Liz shouted to her friend. "Let him go."

"But he still hasn't told you anything," Scarlett argued.

"He told her to talk to her father," Henry said as Scarlett walked back to their group. Yes, he had. Her father who had refused to call the police, who had let his new wife block Liz's attempts to speak to him in the aftermath. Could she really expect to get more from him than Dorian had given?

"He was just saying that to get away. And look, there he goes." Dorian had wasted no time reversing out of his spot and pulling onto the main road. It seemed Scarlett really had put the fear of God into him.

"No," Liz said, her voice shaky. "I believe him."

A sinking, falling feeling took over Liz. She already knew this would be a lost cause, but still...

She had to try.

CHAPTER 21

LIZ WATCHED DORIAN DEPART FOR A SECOND TIME IN THE span of just ten minutes. Why did he go through all the effort of tracking her down today if he still didn't want to tell her the full truth? She wished she could go back to trusting the people in her life, but it felt as if everyone was suspect now. Was there anyone left she could trust?

"Are you going to be okay?" Scarlett hung an arm over Liz's shoulder, reminding her that at least her friends would never hurt her. She'd always thought that about her father, too. And now...

"I don't know. I can't stop thinking about what he said. That my father knows this secret, whatever it is."

"Henry? Give us a minute?" Scarlett said to her fiancé before leading Liz back toward the car. She climbed into the passenger seat and handed Liz the keys. "Go talk to him. Do it now. Like ripping off a Band-Aid."

"But Henry—?"

"Won't mind if I blow him off, if that's what you want." Scarlett's breaths came out labored. She was frightened for Liz, just as much as Liz was for herself. "Do you want me to come with you to talk to your dad?"

Maybe that was the biggest difference between the two friends. Scarlett put her fears aside, while Liz often felt consumed by them. What if talking to her dad changed everything? What if there was no going back? She shook her head and stuck the key into the ignition before she could change her mind. "No. This is something I need to do on my own."

Scarlett smiled and took a long, slow breath out. "Atta girl. Now take my car. I'll have Henry drop me back at the apartment later. If you need anything—*anything*—call me. I'll be there in a flash."

"Thank you." Liz sniffled, and her friend was quick to grab a tissue from the glove compartment.

"Do one thing for me?"

Liz nodded before blowing her nose.

"Remember that you are you, no matter what. Nothing can change that." These words shook Liz to the core. It seemed she and Scarlett were of one mind, that they both knew this revelation would change everything. But was it possible Scarlett knew more than she'd let on? Liz had to know what she was walking into.

"Do you know what it is?"

"I have my suspicions, but I'd hate to guess and be wrong."

"Could you—?"

Scarlett shook her head. "No, Dorian's right. You need to talk to your dad. Now, are you sure you don't want me to come with you?"

Liz placed a hand on each side of the steering wheel. "I can do this."

"I know you can." Scarlett gave her a quick squeeze before getting out of the car. She waved as Liz drove slowly away, back to the house she'd escaped less than two hours ago.

Liz made it as far as the turn in for her father's street when she chose to head to the apartment and pick up Samson for moral support. Even though she'd told Scarlett not to come, she needed someone to be there for her, to be on her side. The worst part of it all was she didn't know how she would feel about her father once he'd told her everything he'd been hiding presumably for years since she had no memory of Warwick.

Samson hung his head out the rear window and broofed happily when the two of them arrived at the house.

Her father came out onto the driveway to greet them.

"Back so soon?" he asked brightly, the confrontation from that morning already behind him.

"I met with Dorian," she said, slowly unbuckling her seatbelt and exiting the car. She let Samson out from the back, and he immediately raced over to shower her dad in kisses.

The smile disappeared from his face almost as if it had been flipped off by a switch. "The one who called me at the resort?"

"Yes." Well, that confirmed her suspicions on that point. What else would she learn before the day was through?

Her father didn't say anything, and Liz took a moment to examine his face. He wore a steady blankness. The switch had turned off all his emotions, not just his smile.

"How do you know Charles Warwick?" Liz asked, crossing her arms to defend herself from whatever words were spoken next.

He cast his eyes to the ground, and that was when she knew her father planned on lying to her. "I don't."

"Well, he definitely seemed to know you."

He faltered, took a step back. "It was all a misunderstanding."

"Then why didn't you call the police?" She couldn't let him do this to her, not anymore. She deserved the truth, and she would get it, no matter what.

"Please, Lizzy. Please stop asking all these questions. Don't ruin what we have."

"I'm not the one keeping secrets," she answered with a tone she'd never expected to use on her beloved father.

"You don't understand. You shouldn't be burdened with it. I..." His voice cracked, and he let out a strangled cry. He tried to choke it back down, but it was too late, the weight of his emotions too heavy.

And now she was crying, too. She had to remind herself that she hadn't done anything wrong, that she'd been dragged into this situation, that more than likely it was her father who had brought her here. "Daddy, please," she begged. "What happened? Tell me."

Hearing her voice break, Samson rushed to Liz's side and placed his giant head between her hip and dangling hand.

"I just can't. We're already too far gone." He glanced toward the house as if contemplating an escape from the one person he'd always loved the most. Or so she'd thought. Liz didn't know what to believe anymore, and she was sick of all these non-explanations.

She raised her voice in desperation. "I don't understand. What does that mean?"

But her father stood firm. "It means it's too late now. I did what I did, and I would do it all over again, too. It's only because I love you so much. You are my favorite person in the world."

117

The front door opened and Vanessa stepped out onto the porch. "What is going on here? Why are you making a scene? Ben, why are you crying?"

Liz's father refused to take his eyes off her. She wondered if he could even see her that well through all the tears. "You're supposed to say 'in the whole wide world' and then I'm supposed to say 'a million times around,'" he said, reciting the lines from their favorite goodnight game.

Liz stiffened. She loved her father, but what if that was all based on a lie so big she could never forgive him for it? "No," she said. "I won't. Not unless you tell me the truth. All of it."

He sobbed again, and Vanessa charged toward Liz. "Get out of here," she said through gritted teeth. "I don't care who you are. Anyone who would upset my husband like this isn't welcome in our home."

Liz wanted to argue, to say that this was her home first, that he was her dad first. But...

An unsettling thought flashed in her mind, the one she'd tried so hard to keep in the darkness. What if he *wasn't* her father? What if that was the lie? The DNA? Warwick's search? What if...?

Dorian and her father had both told her Warwick was dangerous, but what if he was the only one willing to give her answers?

"Fine by me," Liz told Vanessa at last. "You won't see me again until I have some answers. If he won't give them to me, I'll find someone else who will."

CHAPTER 22

LIZ TOOK THE NEXT COUPLE DAYS TO DECOMPRESS. SHE WENT to work, tried to go about her day normally. When neither her father nor Dorian made any additional effort to get in touch with her, she began to wonder if she should let the whole thing go—if there was any universe that would allow her to pack away all that she had learned and put it out of her mind for good.

But, no.

The longer she went without solving this mystery, the more it would eat at her, drive her crazy. She already felt as if she'd lost her grip on reality. She needed to ground herself in this new truth, whatever it was, and then take it from there.

"Are you sure you're going to be okay without me?" Scarlett said as she crammed another dress into her suitcase Tuesday evening. "I mean, a lot's going on,"

"I'll be fine. I just can't believe you're leaving already. I only just got back home. But I guess that's just the way wedding season goes." Liz smiled, tried to play things off lightly so that Scarlett wouldn't suspect what she planned to do while her roommate was away that week.

"Aww, I'll miss you, too. Hugs!"

Liz loved how her friend both said the word aloud and made the gesture. It was like a double sign of affection, and she needed it, though Scarlett had no idea why...

"So tell me again, who's getting married?" Liz planned to make small talk until Scarlett left for the airport, and luckily Scarlett never ran out of things to discuss when she had a willing conversation partner.

"It's my friend—*hey*, his name is Ben, too—who's getting married, and most of us never thought we'd see this day. I certainly didn't. And his fiancée, Summer, totally—I'm rambling, aren't I?"

"You wouldn't be Scarlett if you didn't ramble." Liz laughed and handed her friend a little clutch of toiletries to pack in her bag. "I can tell you're excited to see your Texas family."

Scarlett gave Liz another hug and said, "You know you're my Alaska family, right?" She could tell her roommate was nervous about leaving her alone in the wake of everything that had happened the past week. Even though things had quieted down during the past couple of days, she must have also sensed that this was merely the eye of the storm. Liz needed to put her at ease, make her feel good about going home—and she knew just how to do that.

"Of course I do. Besides, while you're gone, I'm going to go stay with our extended Alaska family."

"You mean?"

"Yeah, Lauren and Shane said the dogs and I could hang at their place for the week. Sofia gave me the week off, and I figure it's best for me to be far off the beaten path while everything's still so much up in the air." This was the truth. Liz did plan to go to Lauren and Shane's, but not until tomorrow.

Scarlett's lingering tension notably left her body. "That's a great idea."

"It was Henry's, actually."

Scarlett smiled proudly. "God love that man."

"I can see that." Liz laughed again. Now she felt lighter, too. "Is he nervous about meeting everyone in your hometown?"

"I think he is, a little. But I have all week to butter them up. He'll fly down after his exams on the day before the wedding."

"Sounds like you've thought of everything."

"Naturally." Scarlett placed a hand on each of her hips and surveyed the room. When she was satisfied with her packing efforts, she turned the full force of her gaze on Liz. "Look, Liz... Ben's my friend, but you're my best friend. It's not too late for me to cancel the flight and stay here to help you."

"There's nothing to help with. Until either Dorian or my father is willing to talk to me, I don't really have any options." The last thing Liz wanted to do was reveal her actual plan for that evening. Her friend needed some time to get back to her Texas roots—and Liz needed her out of the way in case anything truly dangerous went down.

"See you in just over a week, okay?"

"Call me when you get there."

"I will."

Liz waited a few minutes to make sure Scarlett had fully departed and didn't need to come back for any forgotten luggage, then she texted Lauren.

Still okay for me to come stay with you for the week?

Of course! Are you leaving now?

I'll be there tomorrow. Late, probably.

Briar Rose will be so psyched to see the dogs, and I'm psyched to see you!

Liz smiled, then dropped her phone into her purse.

Technically, she hadn't lied to anyone, but she'd also worked very hard to keep her plans for the evening secret. She would go to Lauren's that night, but first...

She was going to see Warwick.

CHAPTER 23

WHO AM I?

What am I to you?

When did we last meet?

Why are you only looking for me now?

How come I can't remember?

These were the questions that ran through Liz's mind as she drove toward the hotel downtown. The whispers of answers all warned her to stay away from Warwick, but at this point, he seemed to be the only one willing to offer information.

They said he was dangerous, but he hadn't hurt her despite the flurry of punches and kicks she'd sent his way. He'd been alone with Victoria for hours in that very same room but hadn't hurt her, either.

What if Warwick was the good guy in all of this? What

if he was just misunderstood the way Scarlett's fiancée Henry had been?

She parked on the curb, and the gusting wind slammed her door shut behind her almost as if the very hand of God had decided to aid her in this mission. She stood on the sidewalk, staring back at her car. It wasn't too late to change her mind, to drive away toward Puffin Ridge and the safety of Lauren and Shane's country cabin.

But it was too late—too late to go back to who she'd been before the desperate need to know consumed her. She was a husk of who she'd been, a ghost.

Only the truth could return her to life.

"Is everything okay, miss?" a bellhop asked, peeking his head out through the glass entryway.

Liz ducked her head and smiled shyly. "Yes, I've just come to see my father, but I forgot what room he's staying in."

Father. *Her father.* Someone other than Ben Benjamin. She hated it, but even as she said the words to this perfect stranger, she knew they had to be true.

The bellhop smiled. "C'mon in. The front desk can help you find him in a jiff."

This was it.

She lifted her head high and marched into the hotel's lobby. She didn't even remember speaking with the concierge, but now she was getting onto the elevator.

Now she was exiting on the fourth floor.

Now she was standing in front of his door.

Could this be the last thing she ever did?

What if he hurt her? Kidnapped her and took her away from all she'd ever known?

What if he was kind and placid and told her the truth like she wanted, but it was a truth she couldn't handle?

Who would she be when she finally found out?

What would she do?

Liz closed her eyes and raised her fist to the door. Knocked.

She'd expected to hear a shuffling, hurried footsteps, to see his look of surprise and relief when he opened the door to her. But the only sound came from the buzzing lights overhead, the only sight when at last she opened her eyes was the worn paint on the door and the outdated wallpaper pattern that flanked it on either side.

She took a deep breath and knocked again. And again. And again.

Harder, louder.

Knock, knock, knock.

Her knuckles pulsed with pain, her heart sped at an exhilarating pace. But no one answered the door.

Now what?

CHAPTER 24

LIZ WAITED IN THE LOBBY FOR MORE THAN AN HOUR, HOPING it wasn't too late to catch Warwick that evening. As she did, she skimmed through hundreds of pages of search results, hoping the next link would lead her to the "Charles Warwick" she knew. Most linked to a man who had died in the eighteen-hundreds. None matched the man she had met on two separate occasions now.

In the end, her Internet sleuthing proved just as fruitless as her hotel stakeout. Warwick didn't show, and she learned nothing new to aid in her investigation. Finally, Liz gave up and drove home in defeat.

She thought back to the way the wind had slammed her door, how she'd envisioned the hand of God interceding in her mission. But He had shut the door for her, not opened it.

What if it was a sign that she needed to let this go before someone ended up seriously hurt?

She wished she could talk about it with somebody, but both Dorian and her father refused to tell her more, and her friends would only worry or try to stop her in her quest, especially as far as Warwick was concerned.

No, he was the only one who could help her now. She had to take the chance, accept the risk.

The next morning she stopped by the hotel again, but the concierge told her Mr. Warwick had checked out late last night.

Gone. No more trails to follow. No truths left to find.

Did this mean he had given up on reaching her?

Her heart fell as she contemplated this strange loss, equal parts good and bad.

Liz simply didn't know what to believe anymore, didn't know if she'd ever be able to turn back despite reaching the end of the road.

She texted Lauren to let her know she and the dogs would be by earlier than expected. At least the visit with her friend would help distract her reeling mind.

On the road to Puffin Ridge, she placed a call to Dorian on her Bluetooth, but it rang several times before finally clicking over to voicemail. Had he left, too?

When the robotic voice prompted her to leave a message

at the tone, she did, hoping it would give her some measure of closure.

"Dorian Whitley," she said with an exhausted laugh. "You told me not to hate you, but guess what? I do. I hate you with every fiber of my being, Dorian. You brought chaos and lies into my life. You told me to talk to my father if I wanted to know the truth. But surprise, surprise, he wouldn't say a thing. I tried to talk to Warwick, and he's gone without a trace."

The GPS interrupted her with instruction to "Take exit on right to Glenn Highway, then keep straight for eighty miles to Puffin Ridge." Liz pressed hard until the device turned off. She already knew the way and didn't need that robotic voice irritating her.

She huffed and quickly finished her message to Dorian. "Maybe you're gone, too. I don't know. But what I do know is I hate you for ruining my life, then not even having the decency to pick up the phone."

She hung up before she could tear into him more and hit the steering wheel in frustration. The car swerved from the motion, forcing her to focus on her driving once again.

Liz shook. She was so, so angry, but was it really because of Dorian? He seemed the easiest target since he'd been the one to first introduce her to this mystery, since he wasn't answering his phone now when she desperately needed someone to tell her what was going on.

She tried listening to the radio as she drove along the lonely stretch of highway to Puffin Ridge, but every lyric just set her further on edge. It all seemed to taunt her, to remind her that she'd never know the truth about her own life, that she'd reached a dead end on the journey into her past.

Just as Liz had pulled into Lauren and Shane's driveway, her phone rang through the speakers. Her father calling to apologize? Dorian? Either would have been welcome at this point.

But, no, of course, it couldn't be that simple.

"Hey, girl," Sofia said casually, but her voice shook with uncertainty. "Where are you?"

"Puffin Ridge. Do you need me to come cover a shift?" The front door of the cabin opened, and Lauren waved from the doorway. Naturally, all three dogs in the backseat of her car went crazy with joyous barking.

"No, no. Don't do that." Sofia said something more, but her voice cut out.

"Sofia? I can hardly hear you over the dogs. What's going on?" Liz waved Lauren over and pointed toward the back seat. Luckily, her friend knew just what she was trying to say, and let the dogs out to play in the yard.

"Liz? Are you still there?" The rustling of fabrics hinted that Sofia had gone to hide in the back of the store where they kept overstock garments.

"Yeah. Sorry about that. The dogs were—"

"It's fine. *Listen,*" Sofia's voice dropped to a whisper. "There was some creepy dude here looking for you. He waited for almost an hour before I threatened to call the cops and made him go away. I think he's somewhere nearby still."

Liz's heart sped. She should have waited longer, shouldn't have left Anchorage so easily. She asked the question even though she already knew the answer somewhere deep within. "Was it the same creepy guy as last week? Dorian?"

"The cute one? No. This dude was old—gray hair in his beard and all that. I managed to sneak a picture. Just a sec, I'll send it to you."

A moment later Liz's phone buzzed with a message and sure enough, the image of Mr. Warwick stared back at her. She didn't understand. Hadn't he left? Why was he still looking for her?

"Did you get his number?" Liz asked, equal parts hope and dread filling her chest.

"What? No! Liz, trust me, this guy was *not* here for altruistic reasons. You know it takes a lot to weird me out. Heck, I'm the queen of weird, but this guy scared the bejeezus out of me. I wanted you to know so you could be on the lookout, *not* so you could return his visit."

Sofia clearly meant the words, but she also knew so little of what was really going on. She didn't know how desperately Liz needed to talk to somebody—anybody—who could give her answers.

A sigh escaped before she could suck it back. "Thanks for sending the picture. I've got to go."

This set her boss further on edge. "Liz? Stay away from him, okay? I don't often play the employer card, but seriously, boss's orders."

She simply didn't have enough energy left to fight off her friends. "Okay," Liz answered, then hung up the phone.

Everyone in her life had lied to her, so what would one more lie hurt?

CHAPTER 25

LIZ STEPPED OUT OF THE CAR AND INTO LAUREN'S WAITING arms. How long would she have to stay before she could return to her hunt in Anchorage? She felt bad already looking to form an escape plan, especially since Lauren seemed so happy to see here.

"I'm so excited you're here!" her friend squealed. "It just hasn't been the same since Scarlett moved back to the city. It's so lonely, Shane and I are even talking about starting a family."

Well, this was unexpected, and something easy to latch onto. Lauren didn't have to know about the call from Sofia or Liz's plan to return to the city by tomorrow morning. While she was here, she could play the part of the good friend. Normally, she wouldn't have to pretend. She liked

Lauren, but she just didn't have any more pieces of herself left to give.

"Oh my gosh! Are you?" Liz let her hand fall to Lauren's belly, but her friend batted it away with a laugh.

"No, and I better not look it, either!"

"So tell me everything. Have you...?" Liz's enthusiasm was waning already. She felt terrible about not being here fully for her friend. Why couldn't she enjoy anything anymore? Would she ever be able to enjoy her life again?

Lauren kept on talking. "Not yet. I want to get through at least one more Iditarod before having to take a year off. Pregnancy and extreme sports don't exactly mix, you know?"

Liz nodded. "Well, yeah, of course, but that's so exciting." She tried to make her voice go up at the end, but her words and the way she said them clashed terribly.

Still, Lauren smiled, a woman content with her life and place in the world—a woman very much unlike Liz. "Anyway, that's enough about me," her friend said, her voice taking on a more serious tone, telling Liz exactly what would come next. "What was that all about? Some creepy guy?"

Here it was, an easy out. "Were you eavesdropping?"

"No, but you asked me to take the dogs and I overheard. Besides, Scarlett may have called and told me everything."

"*What?* I'll kill her." Scarlett had found a way to ruin her plans all the way from Texas. There was no way Lauren would let Liz slip away now, and the last thing she needed was a friend following her into a possibly dangerous situation.

Lauren frowned as if maybe she regretted making this revelation. "She just wants you to be safe and, based on what I've heard, she's right to worry."

"Well, I'm out here now. Safe and sound in Puffin Ridge where no one can ever hurt me." *Or tell me the truths about my own life,* she mentally added, trying so hard not to scowl.

"Are they trying to hurt you back in Anchorage? What was that call about? New information?"

"Let's just go inside and have some cocoa or something," Liz suggested, heading toward the door, but Lauren stepped into her path, cutting her off.

"You can talk to me, Liz. I know we're both closer to Scarlett than to each other, but I'd love for us to be like sisters, too. And besides." She let out a wry smile. "I can relate to what you're going through in a way Scar can't. I'm a member of the fathers with secret pasts club, too. Remember?"

How could Liz forget? It was Lauren's own mystery that had brought her up from the lower forty-eight and led her straight to her now husband, Shane. Liz only wished her mystery could wrap up so neatly, leaving everyone happy and fulfilled the way Lauren's had—but she already knew that wouldn't be the case. How could it be with all the willful deceit that had already spanned years?

"Tell me," Lauren goaded, bouncing up and down at her knees. "Tell me. Tell me, tell me!"

"Okay, okay." Liz laughed, but it didn't lighten her stress at all. "This guy, Warwick, he came looking for me at the store and stuck around for quite a while apparently. My boss, Sofia, she grabbed a picture of him."

"May I?" Lauren asked as she reached for the phone Liz still held clutched in her fist.

"Yeah, sure. I guess."

Lauren made a face as she opened the text message. "This him?" She shifted the phone toward Liz.

"Yeah, that's him, all right." She still felt funny whenever she saw this man who was a stranger but also wasn't. What was she supposed to feel? Love? Fear? Something else entirely?

Lauren began typing furiously on Liz's phone.

"Hey, what are you doing?" Liz asked, trying to look over the taller woman's shoulder, but Lauren used her body as a shield until she'd finished typing.

"Bingo," she said with a triumphant smile as she handed the phone back to Liz.

"I don't get it. What are you doing?"

"Look." Lauren's eyes widened as she waited for Liz to glance down at the phone.

"You did a reverse image search. Don't you think I already searched for him?"

"But by his name, right? What if he's using an alias? And that's not just an image search—it's facial recognition, baby."

Liz was afraid to look. All she had done was seek answers these past couple weeks. What if they were finally here and all she needed to do was glance down to learn everything?

"Look at the results," Lauren urged. "Do any of those look like your guy?"

Liz shivered as she scrolled through the images as the cold began to seep into her bones.

Lauren watched at her side while the dogs ran back and forth in the front yard—thankfully fenced off from the kennels out back so they couldn't rile up Lauren and Shane's sled dogs.

"Wait, go back!" Lauren shouted all of a sudden. "That could be him without the beard and like thirty years younger, right?"

Liz scrolled back up and clicked on the grainy black and white image. The screen opened up to a newspaper archive for Charleston's *Daily Register.*

She zoomed in on the face. It definitely belonged to a younger Warwick, and beside him stood a little girl who couldn't have been more than two or three years old.

She wore her hair in high pigtails and clutched on to a stuffed horse.

Liz remembered that horse.

Its name was Mr. Hooves, and it had once belonged to her.

CHAPTER 26

MR. HOOVES. DAD. ME.

The picture had come from another life, one Liz was only just beginning to recognize.

Lauren pointed to the screen with a shaky finger. "Is that you?"

"I think so," Liz answered, gulping down the bile that had threatened to spill.

Lauren clicked on the photo again to bring up the attached webpage. The caption beneath the photo read: *John's Island Girl Still Missing 2 Weeks Later.*

"Scroll down," Liz urged. "What does it say?"

Lauren frowned. "Nothing."

"Nothing? It has to say something. What's her name? What's his? How did she go missing?"

Lauren's fingers trembled. "I don't know. The page is

blank. It's an archived listing."

"What does that mean?" Liz yelled in desperation. "I need to read the rest."

Lauren clicked around on the mobile website until she found a page with more information and read aloud, "*The Daily Register* is in the process of digitizing archives to make content publicly available for local researchers and family historians. Please bear with us, as this is a lengthy and time-consuming process."

"So what now?" Liz asked, angry at the newspaper, angry at Lauren, angry at the whole wide world a million times around. "Do we just wait for God knows how long until the *Register's* done doing its thing?"

"I have an idea," Lauren said, giving Liz her phone back and then extracting her own from her front pocket.

"Lauren, hey!" Scarlett's voice rang out over the speaker. "Is Liz there?"

"Yeah, she just arrived." Lauren turned her back to Liz as she spoke. "Listen, I know you're on vacation and all, but mind doing a little digging for us while you're there? We could use your librarian superpowers right about now."

"Well, I'm not technically a librarian anymore, but I'd still love to help. What did you find? Is it...?" Scarlett continued to speak, but Liz didn't catch the words. Even though Lauren had put the call on speaker phone, her posture made it hard to discern Scarlett's side of the conversation.

Lauren recited the caption, the name of the paper, and described the photo.

"No date, huh?" Scarlett responded with a loud sigh.

"Not that I'm seeing, but my guess is it's from the early nineties. Think you could find it for us?" Lauren turned back toward Liz and gave her a big thumbs up.

Now Scarlett's words came across loud and clear. "I know I can. If they're undergoing a digitization process right now, their archives may be a bit out of whack."

Liz raised her voice. "What does that mean?"

Lauren handed her the phone.

"It means it may take longer than usual to find the exact article we're looking for, but we'll find it," Scarlett said. "I'll find it. I promise."

"Thank you, Scarlett," Lauren said, taking the phone back while Liz tried her best not to cry, not to think about the implications of that photo.

Lauren took the phone off speaker and she, and Scarlett exchanged a few more mumbled words before she hung up the phone and tromped around the car to grab Liz's luggage.

"That was kind of a massive bombshell. What am I supposed to do now?" Liz asked as she followed Lauren toward the cabin.

"We are going to have some fun. Get your mind off

things," Lauren answered as she worked the suitcase up the porch steps. "We both know Scarlett well enough to know she'll drop everything until she finds the answers hidden within that article. Until then, we just need to pass the time."

"How so?" Liz wanted to know.

Lauren turned, a dull twinkle in her eyes. "Let's go for a sled ride."

Even though her father officiated the races and her two closest friends had both run the Iditarod, Liz had never found dog sledding all that interesting.

Right now, though, it seemed to be exactly what she needed.

CHAPTER 27

AFTER A BRIEF VISIT WITH SHANE, LIZ FOLLOWED LAUREN to the she shed that served as both her office and his storage room. Part of the reason she'd never liked the sport was that it required so much technical expertise. To her, that took the fun out of just being with the dogs. She also hated bossing them around, even though the dogs enjoyed it.

That much was obvious as Lauren hooked them onto the line.

"So, where's the sled?" Liz asked as she helped double-check each harness.

"With the snow." Lauren chuckled. "As in, not here. Not today. We only use the sleds when we're racing—not so much when training—and this is training season."

Liz stared at the strange setup—a large four-wheeler

hooked up with a huge dog line. Twenty dogs pulled the line taut and were jumping and barking for joy. She'd never ridden like this before, but maybe the strangeness of it would help keep her mind occupied. Maybe the dogs would pull them so fast it would feel like she was flying away from her problems, leaving them all behind.

Lauren raised an eyebrow before coming back around to Liz's side. "You know, with as long as you've been around the sport, you haven't learned much, have you?"

"I know a bit. But not that *mush*," Liz answered reflexively, using one of her dad's old jokes about mushing.

"Wow, that's awful," Lauren said, but laughed all the same.

Liz shrugged. She hadn't meant to joke just then, but it was what she said whenever a well-intentioned racer asked her when she was going to get behind the sled and run her own team. It was far nicer than answering with a frown and saying "never."

"Never mind all that," Lauren chided, waving her hand in front of her face to clear away a small cloud of mosquitos. "Hop on, and hold tight. You're about to experience something that most people never do."

They sat together on the large ATV, Lauren already beaming with joy. She unlocked the handbrake and held it closed. "Would you like to do the honors?"

"Umm, sure." Liz let off the brake, but nothing happened. Not yet.

"Hike, hike, hike!" Lauren cried since Liz had forgotten that part, and with a jolt, the four-wheeler quickly picked up speed. In no time, they were cruising through the woods around Puffin Ridge faster than she could run on her own.

Perhaps if she just focused on all the sensations, on all the steps needed to keep the sled moving along, Liz could put Warwick out of her mind. At least until she could find a way to get to him in the city—or until Scarlett called with news.

They took another turn, and Lauren launched into a story, her voice practically booming in the otherwise quiet woods. It seemed she, too, understood how much Liz needed to clear her mind. To just be.

"When I first started," Lauren said, "I had no idea how strong these dogs are. And—*this stays out here*—the first time we switched from ATV to sled, I kept the same amount of dogs on the line. I knew I must've been doing something wrong, because Shane just looked at me with that twinkle he gets in his eyes whenever I'm about to make one of his famous mistakes."

Liz realized her friend was waiting for her to join in the conversation, so she said, "He lets you make mistakes he's already made?"

"'It's the only way to truly learn,'" Lauren said as she approximated Shane's grumpy voice.

Liz laughed and it felt good, like something heavy had started to leave her body. She knew it would be back as soon as her feet returned to solid ground, but at least for now she could escape. She could fly.

"Well, this speed is all well and good. I've got a lot of control with the steering back here, and there's a lot more friction slowing the dogs down. Sleds are a different story. Almost no friction. No weight to them, either. And no steering. I shot off like I'd been fired from a cannon. We went about a mile and a half before the first turn, and the whole sled dumped into a large snowbank."

"Oh my gosh!" Liz cried as she wondered what it would feel like to fall at this speed. Could the physical pain take away the mental anguish of the past two weeks?

"It gets better," Lauren said, doing her best to keep Liz focused. "The snow hook got dislodged and my boot got caught in it. Those dogs dragged me for another half mile before I could finally get them to stop. I had some serious ice burn after all that."

"What did Shane say?" Liz asked, knowing she was expected to speak whenever Lauren fell silent. She was definitely doing her best to keep her distracted, and Liz loved her for it.

Lauren laughed again, and that happy expression she

took on whenever she thought of Shane flashed across her face. "He said I learned two lessons: be careful when you switch seasons, and always make sure the snow hook is properly secured."

These lessons were nice and fine for Lauren, but had no bearing on Liz. She didn't really know what to say, but luckily, Lauren spoke again before she had to figure out a response.

"It's just the way he is when he's teaching. He's made every mistake out there, but he knows his mistakes only really teach lessons to him. He can't pass that experience on through a lecture or a brochure. Some mistakes you just have to make for yourself. His job was making sure that I would still be around to learn from those mistakes."

Mistakes. Like going to see Warwick. That was probably a mistake, but it was one she needed to make for herself. Just like Lauren and her change of seasons. The seasons were changing for Liz, too, but she had no idea what the forecast looked like.

"Seems like it all turned out okay," Liz said amiably. "You're one of the top racers out there now, and you did marry the guy."

Lauren laughed. She always laughed. Liz hadn't known her when she'd struggled with her new life and the secrets from her own past. She wondered if she'd feel closer to

Lauren now if she had. Right now, she envied her friend's serenity, her easy belonging in life.

"You got me there," Lauren said before switching topics. She could talk about racing forever if she had to. "There are times that we only see people from one angle or only doing one thing, so we tend to think of them that way. Take Samson, for example. He's a big, fluffy teddy bear of a dog that loves being your pet. Do you think he'd like doing something like this?"

"What? *No.* He loves just lying on the couch and being lazy with me." Liz was glad for it, too. Lately, she'd needed lots of extra cuddles from Samson, and he was always happy to oblige her.

Lauren pulled the brake and slowed the dogs down to a stop. "Here, switch with me," she said, hopping up and jumping on the back of the ATV.

Liz scooted up on the seat and saw a large, black Akita face looking up at her, his purplish tongue lolling out in happiness. "Samson!"

"He might not be the best at pulling, but he loves running with his friends. Now let off the handbrake, and let's get back home. I'm sure this guy will need a rest."

Samson had never been harnessed to a sled before, but he knew just what to do. He knew just who he was, even though it had been kept from him for all these years. She tried to picture Samson as a true sled dog but couldn't make the image stick. Sometimes you're born to a certain life, but it's not the one you were meant for. Not really.

What if the same were true of Liz? Was she always destined for her Anchorage life, or would she have been happier in Charleston?

And how could she ever know for sure?

CHAPTER 28

LIZ AND LAUREN WORKED TOGETHER TO RETURN THE DOGS to their kennels. Samson laid down and watched, completely exhausted but happy, too.

"Thanks for that," Liz told her friend when at last they headed back inside. "It was nice to have a break, if only for a little while." She didn't have the heart to tell Lauren how thoughts of the mystery had remained with her the entire time.

"Of course. You are welcome here any time, Liz. I mean it." Lauren put an arm behind Liz's back as they walked toward the cabin.

Liz looked over at her friend and saw her face light with an idea. Sure enough, a second later, Lauren asked, "Hey, are fried moose steaks okay for dinner?" She shrugged, but continued to wear a huge grin. "Yeah, it's not the healthiest, but it *is* the tastiest."

Liz laughed and waited as Lauren opened the door into the kitchen. "Sounds perfect."

Lauren stepped into the doorway and froze. Liz watched as all the lightness evaporated from her body, leaving behind only the heaviest part—the part that Liz constantly found herself buried beneath these days.

Shane's voice rose from within the cabin. "Hey, honey. We've got some company."

Fast footsteps crossed the floor—not Shane's because he still needed a cane to get around. His gait was slow and shuffling, while these steps were quick and light, cat-like.

"Nice to meet you again," a familiar voice said, bringing with it the scent of pine and ink. *Dorian.*

"I..." Lauren faltered, still worn out from the run and unable to muster her usual fight.

"Shane let me in," Dorian said with a cough.

"I can see that. Well, can we help you with something?" At last Lauren moved into the house, allowing Liz to enter behind her.

"Not you," Dorian answered and gave Liz a hesitant smile. "But she can."

Tired as she was, Liz now lived with anger, confusion, and betrayal day-in and day-out. If Dorian had come for any reason other than to give her the full story, she would lose it right here in this quaint little kitchen.

"What do you want?" She growled. She didn't care that she sounded like a raged beast. No, she needed him to know that she meant business. That she would fight to the end to defend herself, to find the truth.

"Come to think of it," she continued, "how did you know I was here? Did you bug my phone? Put a tracker on my car? I thought your stalker days were through." Liz let out a bitter laugh. How had she not thought to check for all these things? Maybe it because she wasn't used to living in an action thriller film. Where was Bruce Willis when she needed him?

Dorian drew closer, a remorseful expression crossing his face. Gone was the pomp, the pride, all the things which had made her hate him in the first place. Now he was just a man broken by secrets he had no right to bear. "You told me," he said gently. "Well, your GPS did. In the message, the one where you said you hated me."

Liz flinched. She would burn that infernal GPS the moment she got a chance. "So you thought instead of calling me back, you would just drive the two hours and pay me a visit? What if I don't want to see you?"

Shane cleared his throat from across the room. "Uh, Lauren, maybe we should give them a minute."

"Are you going to be okay?" her friend asked, concern evident on her face as she looked toward Liz.

"Yeah, go." Liz sighed. "But don't go far. I still don't trust this guy."

Dorian frowned, but didn't say anything more until the Ramseys had left the room.

"Well?" Liz asked, crossing her arms.

"I'm sorry. I really thought Ben would talk to you." He really did look apologetic, but sorry didn't change what had happened. It didn't erase his part in any of this.

Liz grew more livid by the second. She didn't like this version of herself, the one that was always angry, that trusted no one. She sighed again, but it did nothing to lighten her load. "Turns out you don't know my father very well. You don't know Warwick, and you definitely don't know me."

"I want to. I'm trying to." He ducked and ran his hands through the curls on the top of his head before looking up at her again, his intense green gaze locking her in place. "I know you went to see him. Warwick, I mean."

Liz eyed him suspiciously.

Dorian cleared his throat before continuing, almost as if he were choking on some invisible object. She kind of wished he was. "I went to his hotel earlier today to offer up a deal. They said he had left, that his daughter was looking for him, too. I knew it had to be you."

"What kind of deal?" Had Dorian possessed the power to stop this all along? If so, why hadn't he exercised it? Why had he let this terrible game of secrets and lies continue?

"No, you don't get to ask the questions. Not yet. Not until I tell you what I came to say." Dorian's voice was suddenly angry. It caught Liz off guard. "But what I don't get is why you would endanger yourself like that. Don't you value your own life?"

In truth, Liz didn't know the answer to that question anymore. These past couple weeks had been a special kind of hell. If this is what life would be like from now on, she almost wished Warwick would release her to the next plane. "You said he wouldn't hurt me."

"Maybe I was wrong. I don't know." He hung his head. His lips moved, but no more words came out.

"What are you doing here, Dorian?" she asked again. "Tell me the truth, or get out."

"He's your father!" Dorian shouted suddenly, visibly thrown off-kilter. "Warwick. He's your real father."

He expected this to be a revelation, but she just stared at him slack-jawed. Now that she had figured out everything for herself, someone was finally willing to talk to her. Of course. "I know."

"So Ben told you?"

"No, he wouldn't even admit to knowing the man."

"Then how?"

155

"The Internet is a wonderful and mysterious thing. Also, I'm not an idiot. I know how to put two and two together."

"I know you're not dumb. You're also not cruel, and you don't deserve any of this."

Liz laughed bitterly. She didn't back away when Dorian placed a hand on her shoulder.

"What else do you know?" he asked.

"Whatever you're about to tell me." She turned to him and tried to smile, to show she knew he was trying to help, that she appreciated it. But somehow she just didn't have the strength to raise the corners of her mouth in what had been an easy, natural gesture.

Dorian smiled instead. It was soft and slight, but it was there. "How do you know I'll tell you anything?"

"Because you drove two hours, because you're here, because for whatever wild and crazy reason, you actually seem to care. Now get talking."

CHAPTER 29

L IZ SUNK INTO A CHAIR AT THE KITCHEN TABLE, AND S AMSON came over to lay at her feet. They both watched Dorian as he paced the small room.

"Can you just stop moving so much?" she asked, pressing her fingers into her temples. "You're making my head hurt worse than it already does."

Dorian stopped, but she could see the unspent energy zipping beneath his skin. "I'm sorry. This is hard. I feel awful."

"Imagine how I feel." She let out an exasperated puff of air. *He's just trying to help. Finally, someone's trying to help,* she reminded herself, then immediately felt guilty for discounting her friends.

He pulled out the chair beside her and sat down close,

grabbing each of her hands as he spoke. "I can't even begin to imagine how you feel, and for that I'm truly sorry. I'm sorry for all of this. I never..." He hung his head and laughed sadly. "I never wanted anyone to get hurt. It never even occurred to me that might be possible."

"I know," Liz said, and she did. She could see the war within Dorian. He wasn't a bad guy. He felt just as confused and helpless as she did. The biggest difference was he could have walked away, but he'd chosen to stick around—to help.

She did her best to keep her voice soft, pliant. "Can we start from the beginning? Please. I'm desperate to know how this all started."

He nodded and sat back in the chair, letting go of her hands as he did. She missed their warmth, but didn't have time to unpack that feeling. Not when the truth loomed so close. Finally. At last.

"I'll start with how I first met Warwick." He took a deep breath before getting into it. "He contacted me through this freelance job board for detectives. It's called the PInternet—like the PI Internet, right? And like I told you before, I sometimes take side gigs to supplement my income. I like being a reporter, but I hate writing fluff society pieces. I want to write hard-hitting journalism, the stuff that sweeps a nation, wins awards."

Liz crossed her arms and waited. She didn't want to be

rude or make him change his mind about confiding in her, but she needed to know about her own secret past with Warwick, not Dorian's career ambitions. If they had met under different circumstances, maybe...

He caught her eye and cleared his throat again. "But that's not what's important..." Another deep breath. "So, umm, Warwick contacted me and asked if I was up for a gig, but he wouldn't tell me much over email. Insisted we do everything on the phone. So we arranged a call and he told me that he needed help finding his missing daughter who he suspected was living in Anchorage, which is why he had picked me even though he lived somewhere else."

"Janie," Liz whispered.

"Yeah, Janie. Which, by the way, is your real name. Janie Warwick."

She shook her head, rejecting the name that had never truly belonged to her. "It doesn't feel right."

"None of this feels right, but I didn't know until he showed up on my doorstep unannounced. He flew over two thousand miles to tell me I was taking too much time and that he'd double my pay if I could get him the answers that week. So I—"

"Started stalking me."

His skin seemed to redden under the heat of her gaze. "Yeah, sorry about that. You have to understand, that much money, it made a huge difference for me. I knew the guy was annoying and demanding, but I didn't know he was dangerous. Not yet."

"What happened next? What changed?"

"I followed you home, and there was that party going on. I fed you that line about Vanessa and a political scandal because I knew you would believe it. While you searched her office, I took some hair from your brush. It was a lucky break that you're a red head and your stepsisters are both blonde." He smiled over at her apologetically. She hated that he'd violated her in this way. Hated that something as innocuous as a few hairs could throw her entire life off course.

"Once I had the DNA sample," Dorian continued. "I left, thinking I'd never see you again, that you'd be reunited with your true father and have this big happy reunion, but..."

"But what?" She leaned forward, as if drawing closer would help the words to reach her faster.

"It was already late that night, so I decided I would call Warwick in the morning to tell him about what I'd found. By then I'd already dropped the hair sample outside the lab. They have this Dropbox thing like at an old movie rental place. It's kind of cool. Anyway..." Another apologetic glance. Dorian seemed to think if he threw in these light asides, it would make the hard truths easier to handle. In truth, they just ratcheted Liz's anxiety to a higher and higher level.

Dorian's eyes widened as he continued. "Before I could call, Warwick showed up at my door again, just screaming, turning blue from how much he was screaming at me. He lost it, and I'm not even sure he knew all the things coming out of his mouth, but one thing stuck with me."

Liz leaned forward again. Ready. Waiting.

He spoke the next words slowly, each one fully enunciated as if it alone held all the answers. "He said he'd never get justice at this rate."

Liz let that sink in.

When Dorian realized she didn't plan to say anything to this, he continued. "And I thought about that, thought if it was justice he was after, why did he hire a PI when he could have gone to the cops? The short answer: because it wasn't justice he wanted. It was revenge."

She shook her head—believing, not believing. "On my dad."

"On the man who raised you, yes. On Ben Benjamin or whatever his name really is. Listen, I don't know why Ben kidnapped you and hid you all these years, but whoever he is, he's not a worse guy than Warwick. Knowing what I know now, seeing Warwick lose his mind on more than one occasion, and you telling me that you've led a good life, up until the last couple weeks anyway..."

Dorian's words came out fast now, dancing dizzying circles around Liz's head. He said much that she missed, but the words that stayed with her most were:

"All that makes me think that Ben took you to help you, maybe even to save you."

CHAPTER 30

Liz couldn't tear her eyes away from Dorian's lips, the same lips that had echoed her own suspicions just moments before. Whatever her father had done, whatever he'd kept from her all these years, he'd done it to keep her safe.

From Warwick. The man who was really her father.

A flash of red in the doorway drew her gaze, and she found Lauren hovering between the living room and kitchen. Waiting.

"Scarlett called," she announced hesitantly. "She wants you to call her back immediately." Lauren's red sweater grew brighter, a beacon. To what, Liz didn't know.

Liz stood.

Dorian stood, too, ready to follow her into battle.

"Do you need to be alone?" Lauren asked, biting at her lip.

"No. It will be easier if you're there."

Dorian's breath hitched, though he chose not to speak.

"You can come, too," Liz told him. "Like it or not, we're all in this now."

"Let's go to the living room. It will be more comfortable there," Lauren suggested. "I'll grab my laptop, too. Scarlett said she'd be forwarding an article for you to read."

Liz watched as her friend disappeared into the back of the cabin. How hard would it be to run away now? Could she leave everything behind and start a new life without ever having to find out what was on the other end of Scarlett's email?

A strong hand pressed into the small of her back. "It'll be okay," Dorian promised.

And she chose to believe that promise. It was the only way she could pick her feet up and move forward.

Shane sat in his favorite recliner, his cane propped to the side, ready.

Lauren returned with her laptop and settled onto the edge of her chair, leaving the love seat for Liz and Dorian.

He seemed surprised when she sank down beside him not at the far edge of the couch, but so that their hips were touching. She needed the added human connection to ground her when Scarlett shared what she knew.

"Are you ready?" Dorian asked, his eyes vibrant and full of life, like a meadow in springtime.

Liz gulped. *No,* she wanted to scream, but instead she nodded. She needed to do this, needed to know whatever she could learn about the mystery of her life.

Scarlett picked up on the first ring, and Liz put her on speaker.

"You're not going to believe what I found!" Scarlett cried, and Liz couldn't discern whether she was excited, terrified, or perhaps both. "I sent the article to your email, but first let me explain how I found it..."

Liz sighed. She didn't want to know how. She wanted to know *what*—and more importantly, *why*. Would those answers be coming, too?

"We're all ears," Dorian said when Liz failed to provide a response.

Scarlett sounded pleased. "Is that Dorian? I knew you weren't such a bad guy. Actually, Henry did, but I also—"

"The article, Scar," Lauren urged.

"Oh, yeah. Sorry! So I called the folks at the *Register*, but they couldn't pinpoint the exact article that went with that picture without at least knowing a date, or a range of dates. Their archives are out of whack because of the digitization, just like I said they might be. Anyway, they told me they're about halfway through the process, and the person I spoke with really wanted to help. She offered to run some other searches for me since the archives aren't public yet."

"And?" Liz asked. She knew Scarlett loved the process of learning just as much as the result, but this was torture. She needed to know now, not ten minutes from now. "What did you find?"

"Well, at first nothing. I searched for missing girl, but that came up with way too many hits. I searched for Ben Benjamin, Charles Warwick—you know, the likely suspects. Nothing. Then I thought I should search for you, right? So I tried Jane Warwick, Janie Warwick, nothing. Then on the off chance, I had them put in Elizabeth Benjamin. *Bingo.* That did it."

"I don't understand. I thought her real name was Jane Warwick?" Dorian said as the rest of them fell silent. Liz glanced up at him and found his brow furrowed, the gears in his head turning but not gaining momentum.

Scarlett's voice took on a more serious tone. She'd shared her research; now it was time to discuss the findings. "Maybe it is, and maybe it isn't, but one thing's for sure—you're definitely *not* Elizabeth Benjamin."

"What?" Liz asked. Her voice felt like thorns pushing against her throat. "Why? Why would you say that?"

"Look at the article I sent," Scarlett said matter-of-factly. Her voice cracked on the last syllable.

Lauren raced over with the computer and placed it on Liz's lap.

"I'm opening it now," Liz said, panic rising within her. She needed to know, but she also didn't want to. She wanted everything to be as it had been before, as it always was. Once she opened the attachment, there would be no going back.

She clicked to open it, and the world stopped.

"What is it?" Shane asked from his chair.

"It's my..." Liz choked on the next word. It was too big, too scary to let out into the world.

Dorian looked over her shoulder at the screen. "It's her obituary."

CHAPTER 31

Liz's fingers trembled as she maneuvered the trackpad on Lauren's laptop. The short obituary was accompanied by a picture of a stuffed lamb. She chose to read it aloud, hoping it would help her gain distance from the words:

"Elizabeth Marie Benjamin was born on Tuesday, March 6, 1990, at 3:46 a.m. at Roper St. Francis. She weighed 6 pounds, 4 ounces and was 20 inches long.

"Her father was blessed with nearly an hour in her company before she went on to be with the Lord. Her mother passed from complications in childbirth earlier that morning. If anyone would like to donate in Elizabeth's honor, contributions can be sent to... I can't do this." Liz's whole body shook with a wave of tears. She cried for her mother. She cried for herself. She cried for all the years they'd missed.

"It's okay. It'll be okay." Dorian pulled her to his chest and, surprisingly, she let him.

"It didn't even give my parents' names. The article didn't say who they were."

"Maybe it was an oversight," Lauren said.

"Or intentionally omitted." Shane's deep voice had lost its strength. Liz's whole body had. She wasn't even supposed to be alive.

"Was that baby me?" Liz murmured into Dorian's shirt. "Was my death faked? Or...?" She cried out again. "I don't even know what questions to ask anymore."

"And I'm all out of answers to give," Dorian said, stroking her hair, tucking it behind her ears. "I'm going to help you find them, though."

"I'm calling Ben," Shane said, struggling to stand with the help of his wife. "It's time he told you what really happened. Time he told all of us."

"But he won't," Liz cried. "He wouldn't when I asked before."

"He will now." Shane's face contorted in a mix of rage and determination. Liz's father had been a close friend of his, someone he looked up to. Nobody had seen this coming, and although it shook Liz the hardest, it had knocked them all off center.

"Are you going to be okay, sweetie?" Lauren asked, stooping down in front of Liz, her blue eyes glowing bright with unshed tears. They were all doing their best to be strong because they knew Liz couldn't be. She'd fought so hard to get to this point, and for what? More lies, more disappointment. Heartbreak.

"I don't know." Liz sniffed. "I... I just need a moment to be alone."

"Of course." Lauren followed behind as Shane hobbled toward their bedroom.

Dorian gently lifted Liz's head from his chest and began to transition into a stand, but she pushed him back down on the couch.

"*Stay*," she pleaded.

"But you said..."

"I know, but if you leave, too, I'm afraid I'll disappear."

He hugged her to his chest. "I won't let that happen."

They sat in silence for a long time. Liz focused on the beating of Dorian's heart beneath her cheek. It was the only thing that felt real.

"I don't know who I am." Her eyes drifted toward a spot in the corner of the room, and her vision took on a blurry haze. "I don't even know my real name."

Dorian picked up her hand and laced his fingers through hers. "I don't know your real name either, but I know who you are."

She forced herself to sit, searched his face for any sign of malice or deceit. But, no, he meant the words he'd said. Which left one very big question. "*How?*"

"I've known you for two weeks, but I knew you that very first day, that very first dance." A soft smile appeared, then widened.

She stared at him, waiting for more.

"You aren't a name. You aren't your family. You aren't even your past." He moved her hand on her chest, and now she felt the frightened rhythm of her own heartbeat mixing with Dorian's strong and sure melody.

"You're your heart," he explained, "and you've got a great one."

"You don't even know me." She dropped their hands from her chest and placed hers back on Dorian's. She'd much rather focus on the steady beat than her own frantic heart.

"Oh, don't I?" He chuckled softly, played with her hair some more. "I know that you kept it together at the wedding, even though your stepmother was making you crazy. I know that you're smart as a whip and refuse to let anyone—especially me—take advantage of you. I know you're brave and were willing to face Warwick on your own if you had to. I know you are kind and fair, way more than those nasty stepsisters of yours deserved for all they put you through. I know you love with everything you've got and that you learned that from your father, from Ben. I know that you're tough as nails, and when this is all through, I know you're going to be okay."

"How? How could you possibly say all that? I was rude to you. Mean. I didn't trust you. Even now I don't trust you fully. I yelled. I screamed. I threatened to call the police."

"Yeah, but I deserved it. And you're right, I should have added your feistiness to that list, but it kind of goes hand in hand with being brave."

She stared at their hands locked together in his lap. Together, they made a fist. Their hands formed a tool, a weapon, and became stronger. Maybe letting Dorian help the way he wanted to would strengthen her investigation, too.

"Why do you want to help me? Why didn't you just walk away once you got paid?"

"I already told you that day at Tozier. You're my perfect girl, Liz, or whoever you are. I don't care what we find. It's not going to change a thing about who you are or how I feel about who you are. And for the record, I gave all the money back."

CHAPTER 32

Liz sat up straight, her back hurting from the curled position she'd held for at least the past hour. Maybe longer. So many things had shocked her on this journey—finding out Dorian was investigating her, that she wasn't really Elizabeth Benjamin. She would have thought that nothing could shock her anymore, but to hear that Dorian had not only refused to work with Warwick but had also returned money he desperately needed for work he had already performed came as quite the surprise.

"You what?" she asked Dorian, clenching her hand harder around his.

He returned the pressure, but kept his voice soft. "I gave all the money back. Well, the deposit I'd been paid anyway. I was hoping it would get Warwick to drop his revenge scheme and go back home."

"And?"

"He didn't agree, so I upped the ante."

She stared at his face in disbelief.

"Finally, he agreed once I paid for his flight and his hotel for the last two weeks." He made this admission with a flash of guilt across his normally proud features.

"But how? How could you possibly afford to do that?" She looked down at his scuffed shoes, the frayed hems of his pants.

He caught her gaze and shifted uncomfortably. A frown marred his handsome face. "It doesn't matter. All that matters is he's gone," he mumbled. "Well, at least I thought he was until I got here, and Shane told me about him showing up at your work."

"Maybe he had just stopped in to say goodbye?" But even as the words left her mouth, she knew they couldn't be true.

"Maybe," Dorian said thoughtfully.

One thing still didn't make sense. "But if you thought it was over, why did you drive all this way?"

"Because I wanted you to know everything I knew, and because I couldn't bear the thought of you hating me." He smiled weakly, and she felt his pulse quicken.

"I don't hate you. I... Thank you for everything. I'll pay you back." She thought of all the time she'd missed from work these past couple weeks. It would take a long time to catch up on her bills and even longer to repay Dorian's kindness, but somehow, she would find a way.

"No, don't do that." He smiled at her. "I'm happy to help. It takes away some of the guilt in getting involved in the first place."

He'd done so much for her. Surely he would accept some kindness in return? "But you didn't know. You—"

"Don't make excuses for me. What's done is done, that much is true, but I don't think I'll ever feel like I've fully atoned for my part in all this."

She reached for his hand, considered her words carefully. Beside her sat a man who'd found her heart while the rest of her was falling apart, a man she'd thought was the villain when really he had been the hero all along. How could she ever tell him what that meant to her?

She at least had to try to find the words. "I…"

A series of knocks at the door sent the words shriveling back up inside her.

"Coming!" Lauren called, hurried toward the entrance.

The cool spring air filled the cabin and a moment later, Liz's father stepped inside.

"Hi, Ben. Thanks for coming," Lauren said, placing a hand on his shoulder and guiding him into the living room.

He said nothing in response to Lauren's greeting, said nothing when he saw Liz—just stared, trembled, began to cry.

175

Nobody spoke until Shane and his cane had tapped their way into the room and taken up residence in his favorite chair. "I wasn't sure you'd show," he said, appraising the other man with a scowl.

Ben hung his head and stared at the floorboards as he spoke. "I wasn't sure, either. I kept telling myself I'd go ten more miles, then I could turn back around. Ten more, and I could run."

"But you didn't." Dorian's voice was steady and friendly. He was still trying to help any way he could, even though he'd already done far too much.

The old man turned toward Dorian. How had Liz not noticed the heavy wrinkles that tugged at his mouth and eyes, or the fierce streaks of gray that snaked through his hair? When had everything about her father changed into something she no longer recognized?

"No," her father—or *whoever* he was—said. "I couldn't do that to Liz. Even if what I'm about to say makes her hate me... Even though I'm *terrified*, I couldn't keep it from her any longer."

Liz sucked as much air as she could into her lungs in case there would be no way to fill them once the truth had been released into the air like a poisonous gas. "Who am I? And who are you to me?"

Her father, too, had trouble breathing. It was as if an invisible pair of hands had clenched him by the throat and decided to squeeze all the air out of him. He struggled for each word, but slowly they came out.

"Your name... is Jane... B-Bingham. And I—" His breathing grew even more labored as he reached the full throes of a panic attack.

"I... kidnapped... you."

CHAPTER 33

LIZ FELT TORN AS SHE WATCHED HER FATHER—HER ROCK—
fall apart before her. Every emotion surged through her as
she tried to make sense of his big reveal. Tried to determine
what she should do next. Should she comfort her kidnap-
per? Should she yell and rage? Or should she ignore the
crime and focus on all the years of love and family he'd
given her?

"I don't understand," she said at last, having decided to
focus on the facts and sort out the feelings later. "Is Warwick
my dad? Is your name really Ben Benjamin? And who was
the baby that died?"

Her father—the man called Ben—began to cry. His shoulders heaved as he struggled between drawing air and letting
out his tears. *"How did you know about the baby?"* he
asked, his eyes and face both red.

"We found the obituary for Elizabeth Marie Benjamin," Dorian answered.

"Stop crying and talk," Shane demanded. "She's been waiting her whole life to find out the truth."

"Do you need a paper bag to breathe into or something? A drink, maybe?" Lauren offered.

"He doesn't get anything until he talks," Shane boomed. His temper was infamous within the sledding community, but Liz had never seen it up close. And she still didn't know whose side she was on in this confrontation between him and Ben.

Dorian squeezed her knee, reminding her that at least somebody was on *her* side. "Take some deep breaths," he told the panicked man before them. "Count to ten, then answer Liz's questions."

It felt weird, hearing her name and knowing it wasn't hers. Could she ever think of herself as Janie? Probably not. But now she wasn't Liz anymore, either.

Ben finished counting under his breath, then shifted back into his story. His words were still shaky, but they came more readily now. "His name isn't Warwick. It's Charles Bingham, and, yes, he's your birth father."

He paused, but Liz didn't know what questions to ask.

"Keep going," Dorian prompted.

Ben filled his lungs, let the air out slowly. "My name really is Ben Benjamin, and that baby, Elizabeth, she was my daughter." He cried out again as the shadow of this painful memory overtook him.

"We can't keep stopping and starting like this," Shane said, though now his voice held a small measure of kindness. "When you begin talking again, keep going until it's all out."

Ben nodded meekly and looked toward Liz.

"Why?" she asked. She didn't need to say anymore. She only wanted to understand so she could decide whether Ben had saved her life or destroyed it.

"Your mother," Ben started up again. For the briefest of moments, a far-off smile flashed across his face as he remembered the woman he'd loved. "She was married to Bingham when we fell in love. She always said she'd leave him for me, but she was so afraid. He was a man with a vicious temper. He'd hit her, push her, choke her."

Ben gained strength in his fury. He kept going without either a harsh word from Shane or a kind one from Dorian. "She was going to leave him," he insisted. "She was. But then she got pregnant with our child, with Elizabeth. Well, he found out, and she told him it was his. She was too afraid to tell him the truth or to leave under those circumstances, so she stayed. She said it was just until the baby was born, then we'd run away, start all over again, be the family we were always meant to be.

"All of us—your mother, me, our baby, and her little girl, Janie—that was you. But when she went into labor, the entire plan fell apart. The doctors couldn't save her, and your sister, she died an hour after being born. All this happened three weeks before your mother's due date, so her husband was out of town on a business trip.

"It gave me time alone with Elizabeth, and for that one hour she was in the world, I loved her with everything I had. I couldn't stand the thought of no one remembering her, so I took out the obituary but I didn't mention our names. I knew I needed to keep it secret because of what came next."

"What came next?" Liz asked, still taking it all in.

"You already know. I took you. I'd promised your mother that we would all start a new life together, that you'd be safe from Bingham. But now it was only you and me left, and I couldn't stand the thought of breaking that promise. Maybe I was crazy with grief, or maybe I knew it was only a matter of time before he hurt you, too. So I took you and ran as far away as I could get."

"To Alaska," Dorian said.

"Yes." The word came out clipped, as if he had no strength left to say anymore. "Bingham hadn't known of our affair, and he didn't know me, so he wouldn't know where to find us. I called in some favors, paid some shady characters, and was able to get you legally recognized as Elizabeth Benjamin. I had all the papers, and it was my name as the father on that birth certificate. I think the moment that baby died in my arms, some part of me knew what my plan was.

That's why I couldn't put his name down, no matter what your mother had planned. That baby was mine. You were mine, too. You may not have been born to me, Liz, but I am your father. I love you."

With that, he began to cry in earnest once more.

Liz didn't have time to think. She ran to him and took him in her arms.

However it had happened, this man was her father.

And she believed him when he said he loved her.

CHAPTER 34

LIZ HUGGED HER FATHER AS SHE HAD DONE SO MANY TIMES before, but this time was different. It was the first hug where she knew the truth and he was no longer burdened with his dark secret.

"Oh, Lizzy," he said, still holding her tight. "I know what I did was wrong, but can you understand that I did it for the right reasons?"

Before Liz could answer, before she could tell him that it would take time but they would be okay, Shane pulled himself up on his cane. The gasps and grunts of his struggle drew all eyes to him.

"Shane? Friend?" her father said, his hand falling on Shane's arm as an offering to help him up.

"She may forgive you, but I'm not sure I can," he hissed, ripping his arm away and falling back into the chair.

"But, Shane, it's okay," Liz insisted. "I'm okay."

Lauren rushed to Shane's side, seeming to understand something the rest of them didn't yet.

"I know you're fine, Liz, but this man, this Bingham... He had his child stolen from him. All these years he had to wonder. He never knew where you were or if you were safe. That's a terrible thing for a father to bear." Strong, rough Shane let out a sob. His entire face grew red with the emotional toll this conversation had taken on him, had taken on them all.

"But he was a bad man," Ben argued, hurt reflecting in his eyes. "He hurt her."

"No, he hurt her mother. And maybe he would have hurt Liz one day, but maybe not. It wasn't your place to judge him. Only God can do that."

"No. You're wrong." Ben dropped his voice into a rattly growl. "I will never regret doing what I did. If he... If he had hurt Liz, that would have been because I had failed to act."

"You failed, Ben," Shane said, standing again with Lauren's help. "But not in the way you think. I had my own child hidden from me. The pain, the agony I endured every single day... it was a thousand times worse than getting my knees shattered by that snow machine."

Lauren shot Liz an apologetic look as she left the room to comfort her husband.

Liz felt her heart drop to her stomach. Had she forgiven too easily? Was Shane right?

Dorian spoke up. "Sometimes loving someone means risking it all. Your father did what he had to so he could keep his promise to your mother and keep you safe. Imagine what he's risked all these years."

"But what Shane said..." Liz ached for her friend, to have his old wounds torn back apart when he'd only just begun to heal. At the same time, she wondered if she could ever heal now that her past was a festering sore on display for all to see.

Dorian rose and put his hand on her shoulder, guided her back to the couch. "Sometimes there's more than one logical truth," he said. "There's more than one way to understand things. Actually, that's most of the time. And in cases like those, you need to rely on your heart."

Ben sat for the first time since he'd arrived at the cabin, choosing Lauren's chair over Shane's.

"So is Liz older than she thought?" Dorian asked when they were all settled.

Ben looked to Liz. He seemed calmer now that Shane had left the room and Dorian had assumed control of the conversation. "Yes. You're thirty-one."

Liz took this in. She'd missed her thirtieth birthday—blown right past it actually. But being older than she'd thought was a small letdown in the grand scheme of all other differences that had come to life.

"How did you keep it a secret?" Dorian wanted to know. Liz did, too.

Her father shrugged as if it were no big deal that he'd spent the last twenty-eight years guarding such big secrets. Even though Dorian asked the questions, Ben continued to address his answers to Liz. "We were new to town. You'd always been a small child. I started you in Kindergarten early to help even things out. You were four according to your birth certificate, but you'd actually just turned seven."

"And nobody realized she was ahead socially or academically?"

Ben never once took his eyes from Liz. "You were a sweet child, a calm, mature child, so no one ever questioned it. No."

"But she was three when you took her. Surely she already had memories in place. Surely she asked questions." Dorian raised both hands to his mouth as he waited for the answer.

"Yes, she asked lots of questions at first, but eventually they stopped. I knew I had to keep her away from anything that could trigger her memories and make the questions start again." He'd started to talk about Liz in third person for the first time during that conversation, and she wondered if it was because he felt guiltiest about this particular part of the lie.

Dorian began to ask another question, but Liz stopped him by placing a hand on his knee. "Horses," she whispered, recalling the brown and white face that had flashed in her memory many times these past couple weeks.

Ben's voice faltered. "So you do remember?"

Liz shook her head. "Not until Dorian started asking questions, and then I saw a photo with Mr. Hooves."

"Your favorite toy. You cried for it every night for weeks. I felt so guilty. You loved horses just like your mother."

Her mother. She'd never know this about her. How much had been hidden about her life as well?

"My... my mom was a rider?" Liz asked.

"Oh, yes. She worked at the stables, competed in equestrian trials, and you were her spitting image. You could ride before you could walk, you know—at least that's what she said. I hadn't met you yet, not back then."

A sense of loss wrapped itself around her and refused to let go. She couldn't get the picture of that horse out of her mind, couldn't stop wondering if it had been special to her and her mother. If she dug deeper, would she find her own memories of her time with her mom? She hoped so. It would be like a gift getting those years back, having time with her mother that she'd never known about before.

"We never rode..." she said sadly. "I wanted to go to the

pony ranch with my friends, and you always said no."

"I couldn't risk it. That was the hardest part of it all—knowing I was keeping you away from something you loved so dearly, something you were born to do. But that's also why I got us involved in the sledding community. I knew you loved animals and thought maybe the dogs could make up for it."

"But I never liked sledding," Liz said, feeling the air rush from her lungs in an unintentional sigh.

"No, but when you were little, you rode our first Akita like a pony. Do you remember Goliath?" Her father chuckled, but she couldn't even bring herself to smile. All her best memories were based on lies, and all the things she'd loved so dearly during her early life had been intentionally omitted by a man who said he loved her more than anything.

She felt the tears spring up once more, but fought to keep them sealed behind her eyes. "I'm sorry. This is a lot to take in at once."

"It's okay if you're overwhelmed. I'm so sorry I didn't tell you sooner. I never knew how, and I never wanted you to doubt that you are the most important person in my world." Ben continued to sit, but she could sense how badly he wanted to rush to her, to comfort her. What had always come so naturally for the two of them now felt like a line that couldn't be crossed unless done so carefully and with permission.

She needed to give him that permission. His choices had hurt her in some ways and helped her in others. He was a flawed man, but he had always done the best that he could for her.

She quirked an eyebrow and tried her best to grin. "A million times around?"

"Even more than that. Always. You were always meant to be my little girl, Lizzy. And I was always meant to be your dad."

Dorian shook his head his voice a refrain of terror. "But Warwick... Bingham... he's not going to give up until he gets revenge."

"If he does, I'll know I deserved it. What I did hurt him deeply. There's no denying that. But he had hurt your mother so much for years. I know an eye for an eye leaves the whole world blind, but sometimes being blind is better than staring down an ugly truth."

Liz reflected on these words. So many people had been hurt, lost. Maybe she could still make things right.

Somehow.

Some way.

Maybe she could be both Elizabeth Benjamin and Jane Bingham.

Instead of being no one, maybe she could be two whole people, so that no one had to be alone any longer.

CHAPTER 35

Liz padded down the hall toward Shane and Lauren's bedroom, leaving Ben and Dorian alone in the living room. She knocked softly before pushing the door open.

Shane and Lauren sat cuddled together on the bed, his head resting on her shoulder. They both looked up when she entered, and Liz knew immediately that big, tough Shane had been crying.

"I'm so sorry, Shane," she whispered after shutting the door tightly behind her.

"I am, too," he said with a scratchy voice, worn with anguish. "I just can't condone what he did."

Liz nodded. She knew Shane's reaction had nothing to do with her, but it still hurt.

Seeming to sense this, Lauren said, "But we're happy to

have you in our lives, Liz. Or would you rather we call you Janie now?"

She hadn't had time to think since discovering her name belonged to someone else. Though the real Liz had only lived for an hour, it still felt disrespectful to continue using the name now she knew it wasn't hers. "I don't know yet," she said. "I don't know which is really me."

"Go find the answers," Shane said, surprising them.

Both she and Lauren pivoted their gazes toward Shane. Lauren wore a quizzical expression, but Liz understood.

"I will," she promised. "That's what I wanted to talk to you about. Will you watch the dogs for the rest of the week? I need some time by myself to figure out what I'm feeling and who I am."

"Of course," Lauren answered. "But please be careful. I know it feels like you've lost yourself, but there are so many people who love you. Us included."

"Yes, both of us," Shane agreed with a sad smile. "Just because I don't agree with what Ben did doesn't mean I wish things were different."

Liz hugged them both, then returned to the living room and said her goodbyes to the men and dogs there.

"I'm leaving," she announced. "I need some time by myself to take this all in." Her throat clenched on the words she wouldn't say. She needed time to herself, but mostly she needed to find Warwick—*Bingham*—in order to complete the puzzle.

Her father rose to a standing position and waited awkwardly without reaching in for a hug. "I understand, Lizzy. I won't bother you while you're sorting everything out, but please call me the moment you need anything or if you want to talk more. I am here for you in whatever way you need it. Always have been. Always will be." He smiled weakly, and she could tell this particular goodbye hurt him deeply.

"No matter what I decide, I will still love you. One bad deed doesn't erase the past twenty-eight years. It doesn't erase what we have." She gave him a quick hug, then turned to Dorian. "Thank you for being there for me today. It would have been much harder without you."

Dorian nodded and simply said, "Bye, Liz."

She grabbed her luggage from the guest room and wheeled it back out to her car. Why did these goodbyes feel so final? Would she really be another person when she saw them again? Would a different Liz be there for the next hello? Or would there be no more hellos? She didn't know, couldn't think about that now.

It was time for her journey back to the city, back into her past. With a quick glance behind her, she put her vehicle in reverse.

The passenger door opened unexpectedly, letting in a

rush of cool air. She pressed her foot down onto the brake and whipped around to see Dorian sitting beside her. "What are you doing?" she demanded with a tired sigh.

Dorian wagged a finger at her, reminding her of the cocky young man she had first met at the wedding reception. "The question is what are *you* doing? And you don't need to answer, because I already know. You're going to find him."

"Who?" She rolled her eyes at him, returning to the version of herself she'd worn on that night, too.

"Don't play innocent with me. You know exactly who."

She sighed again. It seemed Dorian was always one step ahead of her, whether or not she liked it. "You can't stop me."

"I hadn't planned on trying." His smile made her sick. Why couldn't he go back to the sweet, supportive Dorian she'd just left in the cabin? Did he have more than one person living inside him, too?

She placed the car back into park and took her foot off the brake so that she could shift her body toward his. "Then what are you doing here, Dorian?"

He shook his head as if the answer should have been apparent. "You already know going after this guy could be dangerous, so I won't tell you not to. I understand why you feel like you have to find him to find yourself."

"Okay, great. Now will you please just let me go?"

He reached for her hands and pulled her closer to him.

His eyes trapped her in an intense gaze. "You'll find him faster if you let me come with you."

"Are you offering your help?"

He winked and let go of both of her hands. "And my protection. I thought that was obvious."

"And if I refuse?" Would this quest be easier with a partner? And would he even take no for an answer if she tried to give it?

"You won't," he said smugly. "You need me just as much as I've come to need you."

"That's a pretty bold statement." She leaned back in her seat and glanced toward the ceiling before shifting back to Dorian.

"Let's put it in italics, too. Underline it, even." Dorian smiled as he waited for her to catch his joke, then they both burst out laughing.

"Fine," she answered once they had sobered. "But we drive separately."

"Naturally." He grabbed her hand again and pressed a kiss onto the palm, then closed her fingers over it. "For safe-keeping. And in case you miss me during the long, lonely drive."

Liz shooed him off, but felt all her blood flow to the place where his lips had grazed her skin.

It doesn't mean anything, she told herself. *It's not a good time.*

As she watched Dorian depart, Liz couldn't help but reflect on just how true his words had been. She *did* need him. Her one constant in this crazily spinning world had been his support for her journey—even before she knew she'd had it.

Perhaps his silly little kiss could be her good luck charm for whatever came next.

CHAPTER 36

Even though he probably already knew where she lived as part of his earlier investigation, Dorian agreed to follow Liz back to her apartment. He said he'd make some calls to try to locate Bingham during the drive and then catch her up once they reconnected in Anchorage.

Liz decided to help pass the time by do some calling around of her own. First she reached out to Scarlett, who hadn't heard any of the updates since the discovery of the obituary.

"What? No way!" her friend cried when Liz caught her up on the conversation with Ben. "How are you feeling?"

"At first I felt everything. Now I'm a bit numb, to be honest. I just want to find the truth." Liz focused on the yellow divider lines as she drove, a dotted path leading her home.

"Didn't you already find it, though? Isn't that what the whole conversation with Ben was?" Scarlett grew confused. Shane had gotten angry. Lauren pitied her. Only Dorian seemed to understand what she felt now.

Liz shrugged, even though Scarlett was nowhere around to see the gesture. "Yeah, but I guess I still need to figure out where I fit into all of this, discover the real me."

"That makes sense. Is there anything I can do to help?"

"I really need to do this by myself." She decided not to mention her search for Bingham or the fact that Dorian was along for the ride. "How is everything back home?"

Scarlett laughed. "A bit chaotic, to be honest. The church was taken over by termites, and my friend's fiancée's crazy aunt insists on her bird being ring bearer. It's like a circus instead of a wedding."

"Sounds like a nightmare," Liz said even though the antics of a wedding gone off the rails paled in comparison to her own waking nightmare.

Scarlett continued to giggle. Liz wondered what being home did for her friend. Did she feel like a different person in Texas versus Alaska? Did everyone have more than a single self?

"It's kind of fun, actually, but don't tell Ben or Summer I said that!"

"Deal," Liz said with a smile. She glanced down at the neon clock in her dashboard. More than an hour had passed during her call with Scarlett, and she still had at least one more to make before hitting the city. "Listen," she told her friend, cutting off the stream of ongoing giggles. "I need to go. Talk soon."

The moment they hung up, Liz placed another call, this time to Sofia.

"Are you driving?" Sofia asked, a harsh note in her voice. What an abrupt from bubbly Scarlett.

"Yeah, you're on Bluetooth."

Sofia groaned before letting up. "Okay. As long as you're being safe."

"I hadn't realized you're such a matronly type," Liz teased.

Sofia didn't defend herself and didn't offer any further explanation for her warning, which made Liz even more uncomfortable about what came next.

"So," Liz began, knowing the next part of their conversation may not go down easy. "That guy who came looking for me, did he leave his number or any way to contact him?"

"What? Liz, *no*. I told you to stay away from that psycho!" Sofia yelled. Sofia never yelled. At least not in Liz's presence.

"It's not a big deal. I'm just trying to find out what he wanted." She tried to sound nonchalant, but her boss and friend was not having it.

She sighed so loud and long, it had to be for dramatic

effect. "Have you learned nothing from our favorite horror movies? You never go searching for the killer alone!"

"First off, he's not a killer." Liz didn't know for sure, but was hoping that was correct. "Second, I'm not going alone. Dorian is coming with me."

And now Sofia laughed at her—not in a light, happy way, but with a bitter, disbelieving lilt. "Dorian? That other creepy guy who came by the store? Really, Liz?"

"What? Maybe I misjudged him, and maybe you've misjudged the other guy." Liz felt her own anger rising. How dare Sofia judge Dorian. It didn't matter that Liz had done the same thing herself. She knew better now, and she didn't appreciate Sofia's accusations.

"I sincerely doubt that," her boss said with another long sigh.

Liz either needed to get the information she'd requested or to end this heinous call. "Well, do you have any more information for me or not? Number? Address? Did he come by again?"

"No, and even if I did, I wouldn't help with this madness. I can't believe you're collecting psycho stalker guys like they're Funko POP figurines. How many more do you need to add to your collection before you'll be satisfied?"

Liz's voice dropped to a low hiss, a snake uncoiling like the one around Sofia's forbidden fruit tattoo. "That's not fair, and you know it."

"Darling, I'm the fairest of them all, and don't you forget it." Liz could picture Sofia fluffing her hair as she said this. She wondered what color it was today, since her boss's hair changed just about as often as her mood. At least she would likely be back to her usual self by the time Liz turned up for work again. Still, their fights—when they had them—were brutal.

"Okay then, buh-bye."

Liz hung up before Sofia could give her another earful.

A half hour later, she and Dorian pulled up to her apartment building. She parked and waited for him to walk over to her door.

"Let's take mine," he said.

"You sure?"

"Positive." He flashed a debonair smile and opened her door for her as if she were Cinderella exiting her coach.

At his car, he again opened the door and waited for her to climb up into the cab. Sofia was wrong about Dorian, just like Liz had once been. He wasn't a psycho, merely misunderstood.

Could the same be true of Bingham?

CHAPTER 37

THE LAST TIME LIZ RODE IN DORIAN'S TRUCK HAD BEEN when she'd first learned of Bingham's existence. The mysterious old man had tricked her stepsister into a fake modeling shoot to draw Liz out. Was his sudden disappearance another game, or had he truly accepted Dorian's deal?

"Do you think he left town? Went back to Charleston?" Liz asked.

"I honestly don't know," Dorian said with a frown as if it pained him not to have all the answers for her. "I'm not even sure he lives in Charleston anymore. The number he always used to call me had an Iowa area code."

"So he could literally be anywhere?" Liz sank back against the seat, trying so hard not to lose hope... but they were searching for a needle in a haystack here.

Dorian sighed. He seemed to be thinking the same thing.

"I called the hotel on the way over. He still hasn't checked back in. I asked under the name of Bingham, too. No dice."

"So where does that leave us?" she wanted to know.

"I doubt we'll find him just driving around aimlessly like this. But I also know how important it is to know you're trying even if the odds seem impossible."

Liz nodded. He really did understand her. She wondered if something had happened in his past that had led him to these realizations. And if he understood what she felt now, could he help her figure out what came next.

She had to check. "If we don't find him, what do I do next? Do I give up the search? Try to go back to living a normal life?"

He took a left turn onto C Street, keeping his eyes fixed on the sparse traffic ahead. "Let's be honest, your life was never really normal. Even when you thought it might be, all this stuff was still true. It was just beneath the surface, is all."

"That's not reassuring." She closed her eyes and laid her face against the side window.

"It's not meant to be. And if you don't find him here, we'll find the answers somewhere else."

She sat up straight, excited by what he'd hinted. "Charleston, you mean?"

"I was thinking that, yeah." He turned to her and smiled.

She smiled back. "You said *we*."

"And I meant we. I know you're a strong, brave, *feisty*

woman, but even the best of us need help sometimes. Let me do that for you."

Liz thought about that as they continued their drive up and down the grid of streets that formed the city. Dorian had offered time and again to help, and she felt more secure when he was at her side. Why fight it? If he wanted to help, then she would let him.

"Okay," she said at last. "Let's go to Charleston."

He let out a huge sigh of relief. "I'm glad you agreed, because I kind of already booked our flights for tomorrow morning."

"You what? You are not putting any more money toward this, Dorian!"

"Don't worry about that," he said dismissively.

She crossed her arms over her chest to hide her swelling heart. Why was this man so good to her? How could she have been so wrong about the true nature of his character? Would they have met and become friends if not for Bingham's search? Would they have been drawn to each other in different circumstances? Or was it possible that something so horrible had introduced something that could, in the end, be so wonderful?

"What are you thinking about?" Dorian asked with a knowing grin.

Liz thought quickly and came up with an answer that was at least partially true. "I'm wondering if I'll go crazy with waiting tonight. It's so hard to stand still when you want to do is run full speed ahead."

"Yeah, I know what you mean." His eyes lingered on her for a moment. Was he having the same thoughts about her that she was about him? This was all so ridiculous, the timing so terrible.

"Don't worry about tonight," he said at last. "I'll keep you distracted."

So much heat flooded her face, Liz thought it might spark an explosion. "Was that a pick up?"

"I've already picked you up, Liz." He motioned around the truck with a wink. "And now I'm taking you back to my place."

Oh my gosh! Was he serious?

He laughed again. "No funny business, I swear. I just want to keep you safe in case Bingham turns up looking for you tonight. You left your guard dog behind, right? Well, I'd like to fill that position."

"So you want to be paid in dog food and cuddles?"

"Well, that wouldn't be the worst thing in the world," he answered with a laugh. "Just maybe leave out the dog food, and you've got yourself a deal."

CHAPTER 38

Liz watched the buildings blur together outside her window. The businesses and tourist traps of downtown quickly gave way to the outdated, unkempt buildings of Mountain View. She normally never drove through this part of Anchorage herself, but whenever she did, she made double sure her doors were locked.

As she passed through now, though, she felt oddly safe in Dorian's company.

A cracked and yellowed apartment complex loomed on their right, and outside, teens passed around a bottle in a brown paper bag. She'd expected Dorian to pull into the lot, but he kept driving. She'd known he didn't have much money, but Mountain View? How could he have ever afforded to pay off Bingham with such a massive sum?

Five minutes later, they arrived at a house rather than a group of apartments.

"This is me," Dorian announced, cutting the ignition.

"Is this all yours?" she stared up at the two-story home before her. It was at least as big as her father's house. Although the vinyl siding showed signs of wear and tear and the porch steps were uneven, a beautiful garden bloomed around the perimeter.

"You seem surprised," Dorian answered, his eyes just as green as the verdant grass in his yard.

"Well... I..."

He laughed. "Relax, it's okay. I'm just teasing you."

She did just that as he grabbed her suitcase from the trunk and headed up the steps. They had the next steps of their search planned out. Tonight she could rest, knowing that all the biggest questions had already been answered.

"It was my grandparents' house," Dorian explained as he paused on the porch and waited for her to catch up. "They lived here from the time it was built. A couple years back Grandpa died, and Grandma got moved to assisted living. My family wanted to let it go to foreclosure, but there were too many memories here to just give up."

"And now it's all yours." Liz looked at the neighboring houses with their yellowed lawns and broken toys scattered across the yards. Dorian's home didn't look like it belonged.

He didn't look like he belonged, yet he seemed so at ease, so proud of his home.

"Now it's mine. Well, I do have an occasional roommate. His name is Travis, and he's just as likely to show up for the night as not. Usually sleeps on the couch. Don't worry, he won't come tonight. Already texted me."

"The garden is beautiful," she said, taking in the rainbow of colors and wondering why she'd never learned to identify the various blooms.

Dorian blushed, the fresh pink in his cheeks sharpening the greenness of his eyes. "Thanks. I've worked hard on it. Whenever I get writer's block or don't have enough side gigs to keep me busy, I come out here to weed and plant and to just be among the weeds. Pretty weird, huh?"

She shook her head. "No, I understand completely. Just because you have a rundown house in a bad neighborhood doesn't mean you can't have something beautiful all your own."

"*Ouch.*" He lifted a hand to his chest and took on a pained expression, as if she'd literally broken his heart.

The last thing she wanted to do was hurt him when he had gone to such lengths to help heal her. "I didn't mean..."

He laughed and shook his head. "Yeah, just teasing again. Sorry, I'll stop. And, hey, I'm glad you like it. Just wait until you see the inside."

Liz followed Dorian through the front door and into a

massive living room decked out with floral couches and honey wood paneling along the walls.

"I'm guessing you can tell this was my grandma's place?" he asked with a subtle raise of his eyebrow.

The mid-century modern decor reminded her of the old people's houses she'd seen on sitcoms. She'd never known her grandparents, real or otherwise, but now wasn't the time to get into that. "Well..."

Dorian beamed proudly. "That's what I love about it."

She hadn't pictured him for the sentimental type or for a grandma's boy, but she nodded as he shared some of his memories of her.

"Memories are a hard thing, you know?" he said, motioning for her to take a seat on the flowery sofa. "Sometimes they haunt you. Sometimes they slip through your fingers. Sometimes they're all that keep you going. My grandma was my best friend growing up. I always loved coming to her house. It was like another world where my problems at home didn't exist. Now my grandma doesn't even know who I am most days."

"Oh Dorian, I'm so sorry." She wondered how many tears he had shed over his own loss, whether she was actually lucky that Bingham was still alive and in his right mind. It meant they still had a chance. Dorian had run out of chances with his grandmother.

He smiled wistfully. "It's okay. I'm thankful for all the

time we had together before her Alzheimer's set in. Even if she doesn't have our memories anymore, I do. I keep them safe for the both of us."

"Is that what you think my father did? With my early memories?"

"I don't know, but I like to think so. Don't you?"

"Yes," she said, answering his question as well as the ones that had been floating about in her own mind all afternoon. "Yes, I do."

CHAPTER 39

Liz slept fitfully that night. Although Dorian had prepared a comfortable bed for her in his guest room, her newly unearthed memories rose from their graves like zombies.

The horses.

Their old ranch-style house.

Even her mother. Smiling. Laughing. Alive.

Dorian had said he'd wake her if Bingham got in contact, but she didn't see or hear from him until he came to her room the next morning.

"I come bearing gifts," he called through the hollow-core door. "Well, actually breakfast."

"Come in!" she called, pulling herself into a cross-legged position and lifting the comforter up to her armpits to hide the fact she wasn't wearing a bra.

Dorian held two old-fashioned milkshake glasses with gleaming metal spoons jabbing out from the top. "Parfaits," he explained. "Berries from the garden, and yogurt from the Red Apple."

"Thanks," she said, only realizing then how hungry she'd grown running from the thoughts that had haunted her all night.

Dorian hovered by her bed but didn't sit. "We need to leave for the airport in about half an hour. I wanted to let you sleep as long as possible, but yeah. If you want a shower, better hop in now."

Liz needed far more than half an hour to tame her frizzy red mane. She'd go without for the day. Besides, if she stunk, then all the better for keeping romance at bay while they dealt with far more important matters—like the very foundation of her life.

But what could be more important than love? a small voice from within asked, and she wondered if it were her mother's—if that voice inside had always belonged to her mom, and she'd only just remembered now.

"I'll just be in the living room," Dorian said after taking a spoonful of his own parfait. "Come down when you're ready to go."

Liz watched him pad away, noticing for the first time how nice he looked from behind. Okay, so maybe she would take that shower after all.

When she at last appeared downstairs, Dorian stood waiting at the door, jangling his keys in hand.

"Sorry," she mumbled. He had to know that all her extra primping and preening was for him—a fact which embarrassed her greatly.

"It's okay," he said with a knowing grin. "I'll drive fast."

Fortunately, they managed to make it to the airport just as the boarding for their flight had begun. She still didn't know how he'd managed to afford their tickets, and the question rose again as the air hostess seated them in business class.

"Dorian," she said, angered but also secretly grateful for the extra leg room. "How did you even afford this? And why business class when coach would have been perfectly fine?"

"Okay, you got me," he admitted from his seat next to the aisle. He'd been insistent on her settling in by the window so she could see Charleston in all its glory when the plane descended. "I didn't book this flight. Somebody else did."

"Bingham?" Had he really held back this vital information from her? Did Bingham know they were coming for him?

"No, your dad." He flashed her a wicked grin. "Or, actually, Vanessa."

Liz had hardly thought of her evil stepmother in the last week, but she also couldn't believe a woman who hated her so much would pull out all the stops to ensure her comfort like this.

"*Dorian,*" she warned with a scowl. "Please be honest with me."

"Lying to you in the beginning was hard enough. It's not something I want to do anymore. Ever."

"Then what's the deal with this flight?"

He shrugged and stretched his legs as far in front of him as they'd go—as if to say *Yeah, I got help from the enemy, but look how comfy it is!*

"I told you," he said with a shrug now. "Vanessa booked it for us."

"Okay, you're going to need to explain that one."

He laughed and let down his seat-back table in one fluid motion. Everything seemed to excite him as if he'd never been on a plane before. Perhaps he hadn't. "I know. It surprised me, too. So I called Ben when we were both driving back to the city, and I told him about us trying to find Bingham."

"Why would you do that? Didn't it hurt him to know I'm searching for my real dad?"

Dorian frowned as if she'd said something to upset him. "First off, I don't think real and biological mean the same thing—and I don't think Ben sees it that way, either. Second, he said he understood and wanted to help, even if it was from a distance. That's kind of what I was hedging my bets on when I asked for his number."

"When did you—?"

"When you went to talk to Lauren and Shane in their bedroom."

Her jaw dropped to her chest. She hadn't realized Dorian was scheming in the other room as she was creating schemes of her own. What a pair they were turning out to be!

"Yeah, I'm a sneaky one, but you knew that already. What you don't know is that your dad gave me a list of addresses and places to check out once we're in Charleston. He basically gave us a full itinerary, so we're not searching blind." His chest puffed with pride at having approached their trip so intelligently. She'd give him a hard time if she weren't so grateful for all he'd managed to do for them in such a short time.

One thing still didn't make sense. Her father had come to the cabin alone. "And where does Vanessa factor into all of this?"

"Well, when Ben emailed the tickets over later, I could see they'd been paid for by her frequent flyer miles and that she had chosen to use more to upgrade us."

At the wedding, her dad had said Vanessa liked her too well. Could that actually be true? Well, this was the first thing to suggest it, and Liz still had a hard time believing it. She shook her head at Dorian, insistent that it was her dad who had paid. That made sense. "Yeah, but he could have been using her account."

Dorian popped his table back into the seat in front of him and turned toward her, his cheek resting against the chair. "Maybe. But isn't it nice to believe the best in people sometimes?"

Who was this man? Every time she thought she'd figured him out, he'd go and say something like that. It seemed impossible that the Dorian Whitley she'd met at the wedding could be the same Dorian Whitley that brushed his fingers over the back of her hand now. That smiled at her and caused her to smile back. That made her heart soar higher than any plane ever could.

Moments later, the jet began to roll across the runway, and Liz checked her seatbelt to make sure it was firm across her lap. Once they were in the sky, Dorian unlatched his belt and turned to her again. He'd clearly been waiting for this moment.

"Our flight is going to be a long one," he explained, squeezing her hand tight. She hadn't even realized they'd still been holding onto each other. "So what can you tell me about yourself in, oh, ten hours?"

Ten hours getting to know Dorian better. Hearing his secrets now that he'd learned all of hers. It would go by in no time at all.

CHAPTER 40

THE SUN HAD JUST BEGUN TO SET AS THEY FLEW OVER Charleston Harbor. The sky released brilliant shades of purple, pink, and orange, enveloping the plane the moment it dropped beneath the clouds.

Liz was glad Dorian had insisted she take the window seat, because she would have regretted missing this. It was as if the entire city had put on this display to welcome her home.

"So does any of it seem familiar yet?" Dorian asked while they waited for her bag at the luggage claim.

"Like maybe I once took this journey in reverse?" She shook her head. "No, nothing like that."

"Well, the night is young, and we have a long list of places to visit. Where would you like to start?" He pulled out his phone and brought up the notes app where he'd stored all the information Ben had given him.

During the flight, he'd shared that list with Liz. And faced with the decision of actually going to one of these places now, she chose the place she knew would be most difficult.

"Let's go to the cemetery," she said, spying her suitcase on the conveyor belt and pointing it out to Dorian.

"You're just jumping in with both feet, aren't you?" He wore a look of admiration as he returned her bag to her.

She loved the way he looked at her, especially when he was impressed by something she'd done. It had become a kind of drug, surprising Dorian, showing him just how strong she could be all on her own. "Well, you keep saying I'm brave, and I'd hate to prove you wrong."

Vanessa had booked a hotel and car for them, too, which Liz now really appreciated. What she didn't appreciate was the flashy Audi coupe standing before her.

"This is—" *A bit ridiculous*, she planned to say.

"Awesome!" Dorian cried, running his hand over the sleek edges of the car appreciatively. "Sure beats my truck."

"I like your truck," she argued. It was a part of him, whereas this flashy vehicle represented Vanessa. Yup, she'd take his rustbucket of an F150 any day of the week.

Dorian's happiness as he slipped onto the leather seats quickly changed her mind. Maybe Vanessa often went too far when it came to appearances, but at least her heart seemed to be in the right place.

And now Liz knew for sure Vanessa had made the travel arrangements for them. Her dad always rented the same make and model of the current car he drove, said it was like having a piece of home away from home.

Liz smiled, thinking of her dad and all the little quirks that made her love him. She had quirks, too. Much of who she'd become was a direct result of how he'd raised her. He'd encouraged her to explore even though she now knew he'd chosen to hide some adventures from her. Even now he wanted her to find what she was looking for. He wanted her to be happy, complete—and she loved him dearly for it.

Dorian let out a low whistle, drawing her attention back to him. "Built-in GPS. How perfect is that?" He punched in the address of the cemetery, and they were off.

During the flight, Dorian had shared stories of his grandmother, his college days, even his first love. She'd worked hard to keep him talking so that she wouldn't have to offer much about her past. It wasn't because she didn't want to tell him about her life, but rather, she didn't yet know how her perfect memories might have become tainted by the truth of her father's sins.

Now, however, standing in front of the little pink granite headstone etched with a lamb and praying hands, she couldn't stop sharing.

"My sister." She gasped, and Dorian slipped an arm around her waist to support her. "I never even knew she existed. That feels so wrong."

He stared down reverently at the grave with her. "How would your life have been different if she'd lived?"

"Everything would have changed. Maybe my father wouldn't have taken me at all. Maybe he'd have taken both of us. I just... it's so weird, being here. I feel like I've betrayed her by not remembering her all these years." She rested her head on his shoulder and they stood together, joined.

"You never met her. You never knew," he whispered in consolation.

"Actually, I'm starting to now. I remember feeling her kick," Liz said as she let her eyes drift unfocused toward the horizon. "My mom, she put my hand on her belly. She was wearing this shirt with a beautiful black stallion on the front. It was my favorite piece of clothing she owned, so she wore it often. I remember staring at the horse's nose and being so surprised when it twitched. That's when my mom let me feel her and asked if I was ready to be a big sister."

She laughed sadly as the long-forgotten memory continued to gallop forth. "I said no. I didn't want to share. She was my mommy, and nobody else's." Liz used her forearm to wipe at her nose, then laughed again. "What a little brat I was."

"That's normal," Dorian said, using one hand to massage

219

her shoulder as they talked. "I remember being just as awful when my little sister was born, but she turned out okay. Now we have all these good memories together. Even though we were never close, we were always there for each other, you know?"

She felt the tears coming, and she let them fall. How many had cried at this headstone? How many even knew about the little girl who was laid to rest before she ever had the chance to live a life outside the womb? "I don't. I never got the chance to know her, to make any memories other than this one."

"Well, let's fix that now." Dorian sounded excited, and she was grateful that he wanted to help. But how was it even possible? The past was gone. She'd never recover what she'd lost.

"Let's make some memories for you and your sister," he explained when she didn't encourage him to say more.

The tears fell down her cheeks and onto her bright turquoise blouse below. "Dorian, you can't just make up memories."

But he wouldn't give up on fixing the unfixable. "Why not?" he demanded. "Here, I'll even help get you started."

He reached for both her hands and held onto them as he spoke, facing her. It was the same position a couple took when exchanging vows. Yet the two of them were inventing memories—her sister's grave officiating. "Your mother just came home from the hospital carrying the baby bassinet. She introduces you to your little sister, and the first thing you notice is how she has bright red hair just like you."

Liz laughed. She was beginning to understand his idea, and she liked it. "Then my mom whispers in my ear that the three of us are going on an adventure someday very soon, and I say that as long as I have my mommy, I will go anywhere."

Now Dorian added to the memory again. "She introduces you to Ben and says he's her very good friend and he's going to help take you on the adventure. You pack up and leave for Anchorage the next day."

"It's a long drive, but I like showing my sister all the sights through the window. When we get to Alaska, they have a new puppy for me, an Akita named Goliath."

"And if memory serves, you have a great time riding that dog all over the house like a pony, but you also get plenty of time to ride horses, because your mom opens up her own stables right there in Anchorage."

She pictured it. Every word came alive as Dorian spoke. This could have been real. It could have been her life.

"Soon I can't remember any other life, and I start calling Ben Dad. I like him much better than the man who used to yell at and hurt mommy. I love horses best, but my little sister is all about the dogs. Our father gets involved in the sledding community to share this passion with her."

"As your sister gets older, she begins to race. She's amazing at it, and you often go to her races to cheer from the sidelines. At one such event, you meet a handsome but awkward reporter. He asks you to dance." He squeezed her hands and widened his eyes as if expecting her to curtsey and begin an old-fashioned waltz.

"And I remind him there is no dancing at sled dog events. Unless it's the Miners and Trappers ball."

"And I say, we don't need permission to dance." Dorian took Liz in his arms and swayed with her in the breeze.

She laid her head on his chest and listened to his heart. "Thank you. I liked that."

"I like this," he said, spinning her in his arms.

"I could have still had the same life. Well, in a lot of ways the same. We lost a lot, my father and I both, when we lost Mom and baby Elizabeth, but we still had a lot, too."

"And you're still you, either way."

"And we still get to dance, either way."

The dancing freed something in her, made the invented memory feel so real. Now as Dorian turned her this way and that, she imagined her sister and her mother sharing a similar dance in Heaven.

Whether or not she ever got the chance to really know them, she now had memories to fill in the gaps of time.

And that would be more than enough.

CHAPTER 41

THEY LEFT THE GRAVEYARD AND DROVE STRAIGHT TO THE old Bingham family home.

"This is it," Liz said as their car idled at the curb in front of a modest, ranch-style home. "Even in the dark, I can recognize it from the newspaper photo we found online."

"Do you remember it?"

"A little." She got out of the car and walked up the driveway.

Dorian turned off the engine and followed. "Do you think he still lives here?"

"Anything seems possible with all I've learned these past weeks. We at least need to ask," she explained while they climbed the two steps up onto the expansive porch.

They stood side by side as Liz pressed the doorbell. After a series of gongs and chimes, an old woman answered the door. She wore pink pearls and cat-eye glasses like a character straight out of the musical *Grease*. Her hair was neatly coifed but had gone completely gray without the slightest hint of dye.

"May I help you, sugar?" she asked with a thick, raspy drawl.

"We're looking for the man who used to live here," Liz said with a smile she hoped would communicate the harmlessness of their visit. "Charles Bingham?"

The woman shook her head. "No, I don't know anyone by that name. Sorry, shugs."

"Thank you for your time," Dorian said, nodding to the woman before she closed her door shut.

"Well, that was a dead end," Liz said with a sigh.

"It's something we can cross off the list, which means we're that much closer in our search." Dorian draped an arm over her shoulder as they walked back down the driveway.

Liz stopped walking partway down and stooped to run her hands over the spiky grass. "I remember having a little pool shaped like a turtle, right here on this lawn. Mom would pull out a lawn chair and sip on a giant glass of sweet tea while I splashed away the afternoon." She closed her eyes for a moment and relived one of those days in her mind. When she reopened them, she saw Dorian had knelt beside her.

"Sweet tea sounds good," he said, helping her back up to

her feet. "Should we go get some—and maybe dinner, too—while we figure out our next steps?" They reached the car, and he opened her door for her.

After a short drive around town, they found a restaurant with so many cars parked around it, some had pulled up onto the grass.

"This one," Liz said, pointing its way.

"Are you sure? Looks like it will be a long wait."

"But that means it's good, right?" Liz poked his arm playfully and even winked at him. "And besides, we have all the time in the world."

Despite the obvious rush, they were seated right away. They both ordered the house favorite and giant glasses of tea —sweet tea for Liz and an Arnold Palmer for Dorian.

"I think we should try calling him again," she said as they waited for the server to bring out their twin platters of barbequed chicken with a side of homemade macaroni and cheese.

"You sure?" Dorian asked before taking another long gulp of his drink.

She nodded. "I am. One way or another, we have to find him."

"But what if you already know everything there is to know? What if meeting him only disappoints you—or worse —hurts you?" He reached across the table to stroke her hand.

His eyes begged her to be careful with her heart, both where Bingham was concerned and otherwise.

"That's a risk I have to take." Liz squeezed his hand and let it go, dropping both of hers into her napkined lap. "If not, I'll always wonder. I'll always expect to find him around the next corner, waiting for me."

"And that's no way to live a life." Dorian stood and pulled his phone out of the pocket. "I saved his number under Warwick, because you know, that's what I thought his name was. Here, you call this time. Leave a message if you want to."

Liz took a deep breath before accepting the phone. Even though calling had been her idea, she immediately pressed the button to call before she could lose her nerve. The line rang several times before clicking over to voicemail.

"Should I leave a message?" she asked Dorian in a sudden state of panic.

"Might as well," he answered with a gesture encouraging her to go ahead.

The phone beeped, and Liz spoke in a hurry. "Hi, it's Liz. I mean, Janie. I recently found out that you're my father, and I'd really like to meet you, if that's okay. You can call me back on this number. I'm with Dorian in Charleston. Umm, tomorrow morning we'll be at the Golden Meadow Stables, if you wanted to meet up there. I'd really like the chance to get to know you. I hope you get this. Bye."

She finally allowed herself to breathe as she handed the phone back to Dorian. He was her father. He'd been looking for her nearly three decades. He wanted to meet her, too. So why did she feel so frightened by the prospect?

"So the Stables tomorrow then?" Dorian asked.

"Do you think he'll turn up?" she asked, still trembling from the rush of the call.

He shrugged and played with his straw, spinning it around in his nearly empty glass. "Honestly, I've stopped assuming to know what that man will do next. I hope so, though."

"Me too," Liz said, which was half true.

Just because something's scary doesn't mean it's not worth doing, she told herself as the waiter plunked down their meals before them.

They said the truth set you free, but sometimes it felt like the truth had made Liz a prisoner in her own life. Would meeting Bingham change all that? Or would it be like putting on even more shackles?

There was only one way to find out...

CHAPTER 42

THE MORNING SUN ROSE HIGH OVER GOLDEN MEADOW Stables. This had been Liz's second home as a little girl, and she found herself recalling little snatches of memories as she and Dorian walked through the property the following morning.

She had told Bingham they'd be here, ready to talk—but whether he'd actually come, no one could say for sure. For all they knew, he was still searching for her in Anchorage.

He could truly be anywhere.

"You look familiar," a man with a withered face and pristine Stetson said when Liz had given up the hope of finding Bingham there waiting for her. "You wouldn't happen to know Barb Bingham, would you?"

"She was my mom." Liz smiled wide. There were still other memories to uncover, other stories to hear. Eventually, she would find Bingham or he would find her, but for now, she could learn more about her mother's life from the people who had known her best.

The man returned her smile and motioned for her to come closer. "Still is, I'd reckon, whether or not she's of this world."

"I'm Liz," she said extending a hand. "Maybe you knew me as Janie when I was little."

He looked her up and down at this revelation. His jaw dropped, and he let out a chuckle. "Little Janie Bingham? 'Course. It's been a long time, but I do remember."

"We were hoping we could ride," Dorian said, inserting himself into the conversation.

"And maybe after I could treat you to lunch," Liz added. "Hear any stories about my mom you'd be willing to share."

"Sure thing. Let me go find the riding instructor to help get you settled in. Most of our horses here are boarders, but I'm willing to bet she'd let you ride a couple of her mares." He nodded and even tipped his hat Liz's way before disappearing into the long stable building.

A young woman with dark hair emerged from within a few minutes later and introduced herself as Jess Sanders. Liz wondered if perhaps this had been her mother's job once upon a time, or if maybe it could have been hers had things turned out differently.

"Old McDonald tells me you used to ride?" Jess said without a trace of sarcasm.

"Old McDonald?" Dorian asked, with one brow raised.

"The man you talked to when you entered. His name is actually Donald Jones, but we call 'em Old McDonald after the nursery rhyme." She laughed, and Liz liked her instantly.

"Yes, a very long time ago," Liz said, wondering if riding a horse were at all like riding a bike. How much could she have possibly done on her own at the age of three? For all accounting, she was a total newbie at this.

"Well, let's see what you remember." Jess guided them toward a pair of horses that looked like salt and pepper shakers—one was white with black spots and the other black with white spots. She gave them carrots to feed to the large, peaceful animals, and Liz laughed with the itchy hairs on her horse's snout tickled her palms.

"She likes you," Jess noted.

Liz placed her hand between the horse's nostrils and looked into its large, coal eyes. "And I like her," she told Jess.

"Great. Now I'm going to show you how to mount. Watch me and do the same." Jess pulled herself up in one fluid motion, making it look effortless.

Liz had a couple false starts, but she was shortly sitting atop her horse and looking out over the vast acreage of trails and meadows. The saddle felt like a throne, and she felt like a princess born into this kingdom, finally coming home.

They practiced the commands, Jess praising both the horses and the riders liberally as they mastered each new task.

"That's everything you need to get started. Want to take to the trails?" Jess offered, reaching forward to stroke the pure black horse she'd mounted earlier.

Liz's heart practically burst at the idea, even though they'd come here planning to ride in case Bingham hadn't shown up to wait for them. "Could we?"

"Follow me," Jess said, then clicked her tongue and dug her heels into the horse's sides.

Liz and Dorian did the same, and together the three of them were off. Slowly but steadily, the horses navigated the trails. Right away, she knew why this place was called Golden Meadows. Everywhere she looked, sun-kissed flowers and fields created a beautiful complement to the bright skies above. The air smelled sweet, with slight notes of salt from the oceans nearby. Everything felt restorative— like it could clean away the bad and leave only the good. She imagined herself breathing in the crisp blue sky and breathing out the dark secrets of her past.

"Have you ridden before?" she asked Dorian when the trail widened, allowing their horses to walk side by side.

"This is a first, but I like it," he said, his green eyes blending perfectly with the scenery around them. Liz belonged here, and Dorian belonged right here with her.

"Mostly I like seeing you so in your element," he said to Liz with a smile that took up his entire face.

"We're coming up to my favorite spot on the entire property," Jess announced, guiding them up a gradual incline. "We call it Picnic Point, because most of our riders like to bring lunch up here and settle in. There's even a place to tie up the horses."

"Could we stop for a few minutes?" Dorian asked with a raised voice.

"Got a picnic lunch I don't know about?" Jess laughed at her own joke, but helped them dismount once they reached the peak of the hill.

"You can see the ocean way out there," Liz said as a fragrant gust of wind blew by. She closed her eyes and inhaled more of the rejuvenating air, exhaled more of the bad she'd brought with her. This place seemed bigger than any lies, any secrets, any one person—and she loved that.

Dorian and Jess chatted quietly for a moment, and then Jess turned back toward the trail on foot.

"Is she abandoning us?" Liz asked, noticing Jess hadn't even taken her horse.

"Just for a few minutes," Dorian said, standing beside her at the edge of the hilltop. "I asked her to give us some time to ourselves."

"Why?" She turned to him and immediately found the answer in his eyes.

He placed his hands around her waist and pulled her close, saying, "Because I've never seen you so happy, so at ease with who you are as I have today. I want to be a part of that. I know your past is a bit muddled, but I want to be a part of your story going forward. I want to be a part of what makes you *you*."

Oh, Dorian. How much had changed since they'd met. How wrong she'd been about him until now. She wanted him to be a part of her story, too. Even though he said he wasn't in her past, he had been the one to bring it to her. He was here now, helping her sort through it all. She hoped he would always be nearby, ready for whatever came next in her life.

"That's perfect with me." Liz said, enjoying the way Dorian's eyes danced as she said this. She knew what was coming next, but she didn't want to wait a single second longer than needed. Before Dorian could lean in to kiss her, she closed the distance between their bodies and crushed her lips to his.

And in that perfect moment in time, all of Liz's selves converged into one. She was Ben's daughter. She was Barb's, too. And baby Elizabeth's sister. She was Scarlett's friend and Lauren's. And Dorian meant something even more than the rest, because he represented a future she very much wanted to live.

"I think I've been waiting my whole life for a kiss like

that," Liz said, her cheek resting against Dorian's shoulder as he held her.

"Many, many more to come, my dear Liz. Starting in three... two..."

He lifted her chin and kissed her again. And again. And again.

"I could do this forever, I think," she murmured against his lips.

"Time's up, kiddos!" Jess's boots crunched gravel along the trail. Liz found it funny that she was calling them kiddos when they must all have been around the same age.

"Want to keep going or head back?" she asked once they had all mounted again.

"Let's go back," Liz answered. There would be many more rides in her future. She'd make sure of that. But she only got one first day with Dorian, and she needed to make sure she remembered all of it.

"As you wish," Jess said with a bemused smile.

Liz smiled the entire way back. Even when she tried to lighten her expression, she found it impossible. Every time she caught a glimpse of Dorian, she found him wearing a similarly oversized grin.

Two fools in love.

No matter what they found out next, Liz knew she could get through it. The worst truths had already come to light.

Now she was in the process of rediscovering old loves and finding new ones. It was going to be a great day, a great life.

The stables building loomed on the horizon, a dark blur amidst the colorful flowers that flanked them on either side. Liz found herself wishing the ride didn't have to end so soon, that maybe they could just ride on forever—no more pasts to reconcile, no more hearts to heal, just this.

As they drew closer, Liz saw two figures waiting at the fence.

One was Old McDonald.

The other was Bingham.

CHAPTER 43

Liz felt Bingham's eyes on her as she dismounted and walked over to him at the fence. His smile grew broader and broader as she approached. Everyone had warned her he was dangerous, but the man she saw had the beginnings of tears in his eyes as he took in the sight of his long-lost daughter.

Maybe it would be okay. Maybe all the craziness Dorian had seen was just a fluke from the torment of being so close but unable to make contact. Maybe he had repented for hurting her mother and stood before her now a changed man.

"You got my message," Liz said with a welcoming smile, reminding herself that this man had been a victim in the lies, too. He'd dealt with the hurt for years, and that hurt had turned to anger. She could understand that, and now that they were reunited, she wanted to help him heal. "Thank you for coming."

"Yes, I was so excited to hear from you, even though this one—" He jerked a thumb toward Dorian. "Did everything possible to keep us apart."

Dorian put a protective arm around Liz so that the two of them now faced Bingham side by side. "I had to make sure it was what she wanted," he explained, a distinct note of caution rising in his voice.

"And this is what you want?" Bingham asked her, his eyes quivering with tears once again. "To be my daughter again?"

"I'd like to try." Liz reached out to stroke his arm in what she hoped would be a reassuring gesture.

Bingham jerked away, then catching what he'd done, pulled her into an awkward hug. "I want that, too," he mumbled into her hair.

Dorian pulled Liz back to him the moment her hug with Bingham ended. "It will take some time for you to form a relationship," he said. "But I'm happy you've been able to reunite."

"Not much thanks to you," Bingham said, then began to chuckle.

Liz and Dorian exchanged awkward glances and waited for the other man to say more.

"And what's some time when I've been waiting more

than twenty-eight years for this day? We're together again, Janie, and now we can make sure that man pays for what he did to our family." He regarded Liz with a beseeching gaze, and she saw the first flames of anger light within him.

She took a step back, hoping she could make him understand. "No, we don't need to do that. I want to focus on our relationship, not on punishing Ben. I know what he did was wrong, but he gave me a good life and I forgive him."

He shook his head and frowned.

Liz hated to disappoint him, but she couldn't stop loving the man who had devoted his entire existence to protecting her—just as she couldn't help but love a man who had spent his whole life trying to reconnect with her.

"It's not for you to forgive him," he responded. "You said he gave you a good life. That's great. I'm happy to hear it, but he destroyed mine. Kidnapping is a serious crime. He needs to be punished."

"Please don't," Liz whispered. The last thing she wanted was to feel as if she had to make a choice between the two men who both wanted to be her father. "It will hurt me."

Bingham shook his head vigorously, refusing to accept her words or her plea. "But it will be swift. I can assure you of that. I've been compiling the evidence for years, and now that Dorian has delivered the DNA results linking the two of us, the law will be very harsh on Ben Benjamin. Just as he deserves."

"What about the statute of limitations?" Dorian asked. "Surely twenty-eight years is too long."

"Not here," Bingham corrected, taking on an academic tone. "South Carolina doesn't have a statute of limitations. Kidnapping, transporting a minor across state lines, identity theft, and I'm sure a whole slew of other crimes are just waiting for Ben Benjamin now. My entire life has been devoted to the law, and I can't turn my back on it now. Justice needs to be served before we can move on, Janie. Try to understand that."

"Justice, or revenge?" Dorian asked with a look of derision splashed across his handsome face.

"They're one and the same," Bingham answered, then pressed his mouth in a thin, taut line.

"They are not," Liz said, feeling less and less like this man even knew what it meant to love. "I've had a great life. I'm happy, healthy, and have always been taken care of. Ben never hurt me, and he did what he thought was right. We're reunited now, and I want to know you, *to love you.*"

"Try to understand," Dorian coaxed. "She's already had her life stolen from her once. Do you really want that to happen again?"

"What about *my* life?" Bingham demanded. "Doesn't that count for anything?"

"Of course it does. I want to know you. To be a family," Liz said. "But I will not turn Ben in."

Bingham's voice rose. His composed demeanor crumbled away to reveal the broken man inside. "I can't believe this. You really are just like your mother, Janie. Choosing Ben over me. I gave her everything—*everything!* I could give you everything, too. But you're willing to throw that all away for a man who tore my family apart."

"I know it doesn't make sense on the surface, but it makes sense here." Liz touched her chest, but Bingham refused to let it go. He didn't seem to notice the hurt that had taken over her whole body, because something else had taken hold of his—something that scared Liz.

He spoke quickly now, wringing his hands as if he needed to keep them busy to avoid lashing out. A bright red car caught Liz's eye as it pulled into the lot while Bingham ranted with no end in sight.

"I searched for you for years. Do you know that? I never knew that your mother had been whoring around on me, never knew the baby that died wasn't mine. Never got to hold it. The hospital said they'd disposed of the body, but they'd released it to—to that *man.* How do you think that felt, losing two children at once? I was a good man, I didn't deserve any of that. He stole my life and family because it suited him, and you're on his side!"

Liz tried so hard to be calm, to understand how the years of not knowing had twisted this man's heart. "I'm on nobody's side but my own. I'm thirty-one years old, and I'm not some child you can boss around or tell what to think. This is hard on me, too."

She glanced over Bingham's shoulder and saw two figures emerge from the red car. Even at this distance, she knew who they were—and she was so glad to see them now.

"Hard on you?" Bingham laughed bitterly. "You didn't even know until last week. You're not the one who had to live with this for nearly thirty years. You're not the one who was betrayed in every possible way. Your mother was married to me—*to me!* She had no right sleeping with Ben, no right to leave me, no right to take you from me. You are mine, just like she was. And—surprise, surprise—you are just like her."

A familiar voice rose from across the meadow. "You're right. She is just like her mother," her father, Ben, said. "She's beautiful, kind, strong, and too good for the likes of you."

Vanessa walked at his side, their hands linked. She hadn't asked for any of this. She'd simply fallen in love with a man and now turned up to comfort him in his darkest hour.

"You! How dare you show up here?" Bingham yelled, his face turning red. "It wasn't enough to steal her the first time, now you want to ruin our reunion?"

"I knew you'd make it," Dorian said. "Just in time."

Liz looked to Dorian, who simply nodded and pulled her into his arms.

"We all make mistakes," Ben explained, letting go of Vanessa's hand and approaching Bingham slowly. "Yours was throwing your wife aside. I didn't steal her. I simply picked up the broken pieces. *You* broke those pieces by hitting her, pushing her, hurting her."

"You know nothing," Bingham growled, shoving his hands deep into his pockets. "She brainwashed you, and now you've brainwashed my Janie. Well, I have the proof of what you did, and we're turning you in."

"I did not agree to that. I'm not some pawn in your revenge scheme," Liz hissed. "I will be your daughter, if that's what you want, but I will not be a part of whatever this is between you."

"I don't need you to agree. I'm turning him in."

"And if you do, I will never talk to you again," she promised. "We can never be a family."

"Listen," Ben said. "I know you want me to be punished, but I've already done that to myself. For years. I want to apologize to you and offer my help any way you need it. No sin is worth punishing yourself over for the rest of your life. It's not too late to forgive yourself, to forgive me, to let the past go and make a better future."

Bingham laughed again as if the man before him were ridiculous, some kind of joke. "You sound like a self-help book. The only help I need from you is to see you behind bars. And I did nothing wrong. Everybody loses their temper sometimes. So what if I hit her for acting out of line? She hit me, too."

Vanessa shook with rage. "That's not the same and you know it."

"He stole my child. How do you people not understand this?"

"Like you tried to take my daughter to get back at Ben?" Vanessa took a few steps toward Bingham, but Dorian pulled her back.

"I didn't hurt her," Bingham said.

"And he didn't hurt Liz," Dorian yelled.

"Her name is Janie!"

"I'm sorry," Ben said again. "I didn't realize how much this would hurt you. Barb said you barely ever spent any time with Janie, that she was a nuisance to you. I wanted her so badly. I'd made a promise to the woman we loved."

"Don't put us in the same sentence. We are nothing alike."

"Please don't fight over me," Liz said, reaching out to place a hand on Bingham's arm, to show him that she could find a way to love them both. "I just want—"

A sharp pain shot through Liz's face. It took a moment to realize she'd been slapped by Bingham—the same way her mother had been many times over the years. She'd never known. She'd never known.

"I'm sorry," he said, his voice shaking. "I didn't mean to hit you. I was aiming for him, but you got in the way."

Ben took her in his arms and stared Bingham down. "You shouldn't be hitting anyone. That's the point. This all needs to stop now."

"It won't be over until you're rotting behind bars." Bingham shot one more poisonous look toward Ben, then charged back toward the parking lot.

CHAPTER 44

"WAIT," LIZ CRIED AS SHE WATCHED BINGHAM TEAR ACROSS the meadow. "It doesn't have to be like this!"

"Don't," Vanessa said, grabbing Liz's shoulder and holding her back.

"He can't leave! Not like this!" Liz's whole body shook as her tears fell double-time. Meeting Bingham was supposed to make everything better, not worse. He couldn't send her father to prison. He couldn't!

"I'll see if I can stop him," Dorian promised, breaking into a jog as he chased Bingham back down the trail to the parking lot.

"I'm going, too," Ben insisted, but Vanessa also stopped him.

"Let Dorian handle this. You'll only upset the man even more," she reasoned. "While we wait... Liz, your father brought this for you." Vanessa reached into her purse and pulled out a tattered, old toy horse.

"Mr. Hooves!" Liz cried, hugging the stuffed animal in her arms. "How did you—?"

"I found him in the attic," Ben explained as he watched this much happier reunion with a smile. "I never threw him away. He meant too much to you, and I thought you might like to have him back now that the truth is out. Maybe one day you can share him with a daughter of your own."

"Thank you, Dad," Liz sobbed, burrowing into her father's embrace. *This* man was her real father. He was the one who loved her, who would protect her no matter what it cost him—and it had already cost plenty.

Both Bingham and Dorian blurred against the horizon as they grew more and more distant. Now all they could do was wait and hope that Dorian could find the right words to bring the other man back.

"Thank you for the flight and car and hotel," Liz said, reaching out to hug Vanessa now, too.

"It was my pleasure." Even through the thick layers of makeup, Vanessa's face took on a new glow. "I know we didn't get off to the best start, but I do truly want what's best for you. We're family now, and—well—I'd be very pleased if Victoria and Valeria grew up to be as kind, loving, and brave as you are."

Liz didn't know what to say other than "thank you," which she did.

Her father joined their hug, told the women he loved them both.

This was how you formed a family. Liz had hoped to gain a father that day, but perhaps she'd gained a mother instead.

Maybe it was too late for her and Bingham to start anew. Only time would tell that truth. But while she waited, she could make a real effort to form bonds with her new mother and sisters. It's what she wanted, both for herself and for her father, Ben.

Finally, they had a full family to call their own.

And—

A sudden screeching of tires sliced through the peaceful moment. All heads turned toward the sound, but it was too late to catch what had happened. A red mist clouded the air surrounding a livestock trailer.

Mr. Hooves fell from Liz's hands as she rushed toward the scene. Who had been hit? She wanted neither man to be hurt, but her heart clenched at the thought of Dorian's broken body lying in a jagged heap on the ground.

He had never asked for any of this. He'd simply been trying to earn enough money to get by. He hadn't asked to fall in love with her, or to chase after Bingham now when Liz had failed to make him understand.

He had done all of this for her. And now?

Ben and Vanessa shouted from behind her. The driver paced back and forth, crying out every time he looked back at the grisly accident. And then there was Dorian, hunched near the ground. Not the victim, but rather a shaken, scared man trying to revive the other who lay motionless before him.

Charles Bingham. Her rightful father, the man who would trade her happiness to clench his revenge. He'd hurt and terrified her mother. He'd chased her and Ben for years.

And now it all ended here.

She'd offered him her love, and he'd run away straight into the path of a charging engine.

"He just f-f-f-flew out of nowhere!" the driver stuttered. "Lucky I didn't hit that one, too." He pointed to Dorian who now noticed Liz standing nearby.

Dorian shook his head slightly, then attempted CPR once more.

"I'm calling an ambulance," Vanessa declared.

Liz studied Bingham's body, trying to discern what she was feeling now. More than sorrow, she felt awed by the absolute fragility of life.

One man's decision to take her had set her on an entirely different path.

Another man's inattention behind the steering wheel had stopped a beating heart.

Single moments in time forever altered history.

Sometimes things changed in the blink of an eye. Other times there was no stopping what had already been set into motion.

Bingham wanted revenge more than he wanted his family back. Nothing she'd said that day—or would have said in the future—could have changed that.

That was life. You had to live it while the living was good.

Because you never knew what secrets, what dangers lay waiting just around the corner.

CHAPTER 45

14 months later

SHE WALKED ACROSS THE FRESH GRASS WHILE SURVEYING THE land. Although night had arrived hours ago, light still clung to the sky—the unrivaled beauty of an Alaskan summer.

"What do you think?" Dorian asked as he fell into step beside her.

"I think it's every bit as perfect as I'd hoped it would be. I love it."

"And I love you." He swept her into his arms and kissed her for the first time at her new home.

It hadn't been difficult to prove she was Jane Bingham, nor had it been difficult to claim the inheritance her late father, Charles Bingham, had left fully to her. The only people who knew of Ben's crimes refused to report them, and once the prosecutors saw that Jane Bingham was, in fact, alive and well, they closed the case for good.

She still wished she had gotten the chance to know her birth father, but he had made his choice—and God had sealed the deal. She chose not to linger on what could have been, but rather to work hard toward a future that honored what they had both lost over the years.

"Memory Ranch," Dorian said, holding her to his chest as they slowly turned and took in the expansive property. She could hardly believe this was all hers. Now that she'd completed her own journey down memory lane, she wanted to help others on their paths—people like Dorian's grandmother who had lost their memories to sickness. People like herself who'd had them stolen away. People who were hurt by their loved ones' inability to remember, and even people who were haunted by the post-traumatic stress of memories that refused to leave them be.

Memory Ranch would be a refuge to them all.

They could escape the pressures of their everyday life and remember on their own time. Part resort and part group therapy home, the Memory Ranch would use the therapeutic power of horses and the freedom that came with riding combined with supportive counselors and a peaceful sanctuary to recover.

She wanted to help others heal, to remember, and also to learn to move beyond the memories when needed.

"It's really happening. It's all yours." Dorian kissed her forehead, and she smiled.

"Soon it will be all ours." She returned her fiancé's kiss on his cheek.

Just over a year had passed since their time in Charleston, and they would be married in the fall. Soon it wouldn't matter if she called herself Bingham or Benjamin, because she'd be a Whitley.

Mrs. Dorian Whitley.

They'd both returned to school last autumn. She had originally stopped after two years of college, but was now re-enrolled as a proud Psychology student. She wouldn't just stop at her bachelor's degree, either. She loved learning about the human mind and all its hidden intricacies, and she planned to get her Ph.D. even if she'd be forty by the time that happened.

Dorian had already finished his bachelor's degree, so he'd enrolled as a master's student in Criminal Justice. It seemed to him that his entire life had been leading there—from growing up in the slums, to his PI gigs and their tangle with Bingham. He'd learned to respect justice, and his desire to keep people safe only grew as he let more and more into his life.

Bingham had taught them both about the razor's edge between justice and vengeance and how the law needed more people to uphold not only its mandates, but also its spirit.

People like Dorian who had found her when she couldn't even find herself.

And now Elizabeth Jane's memories had never been so sweet, her future never so bright, and her present never so full of passion, love, and life.

As special and powerful as memories could be, she knew now that life wasn't the sum of all the little moments that filled out your days.

It was the people you loved and who loved you in return that made this the most glorious journey of all.

Are you ready to see Liz's ranch in action? Meet Ellie. She was lucky to survive what should have been a fatal accident. Unfortunately, she woke up with no memories of her past or what her life was before...

CLICK HERE to get your copy of *The Sweetest Memory,* so that you can keep reading this series today!

And make sure you're on Melissa's list so that you hear about all her new releases, special giveaways, and other sweet bonuses.

You can do that here: <ins>MelStorm.com/gift</ins>

WHAT'S NEXT?

Ellie was lucky to survive what should have been a fatal accident. Unfortunately, she woke up with no memories of her past or what her life was before.

Recovery is slow, but each night she dreams of the same nameless, faceless man. It's clear she loved him once, but she has no idea who he was or why he abandoned her in her hour of need. And as Ellie's memories slowly continue resurface, she is horrified by the type of person she was before and questions how anyone could have ever loved her as she was.

Will she treat the accident as a second chance to right the mistakes of her past while forging a new future? Or will she risk everything that's left in an attempt to reunite with the man that only her heart remembers?

Join Ellie and Liz at this healing Anchorage horse ranch in an unforgettable tale of new beginnings, second chances, and finding where you belong. Start reading THE SWEETEST MEMORY today!

The Sweetest Memory is now available.

CLICK HERE to get your copy so that you can keep reading this series today!

SNEAK PEEK OF THE SWEETEST MEMORY

Ellie could smell the wine on her date's breath as he leaned closer, bringing his mouth toward hers. Polishing off a full bottle of California Zinfandel on his own had taken this guy from slightly irritating to downright obnoxious, and now he had the gall to try to kiss her.

Thrusting her hand out to him in a clearly platonic gesture, she turned to the side and murmured, "I had a nice time, thank you."

Now please let me leave without either of us making a scene, she mentally finished.

Ellie allowed him to place his hand at the small of her back as they exited the restaurant, but jumped in her waiting car so quickly she almost snagged her skirt in the door.

Her date laughed and pried the door back open, smiling at her the way she imagined a shark might smile at its prey before taking a big, bloody bite. "Oh, c'mon, Ellie." He frowned and shook his head as if she was the one who had done something ridiculous. "Not even a little kiss after I paid for your dinner?"

Unwilling to take her eyes off him for even a second, she blind-groped for her purse, pulled it onto her lap, and pulled out a fifty dollar bill. She shoved it into his hand, shivering as their skin briefly made contact. "There, that should cover my share. Goodnight."

Luckily, the suddenness of her gesture caused him to stumble back in surprise, which gave her the perfect chance to slam her door, press down hard on the locks, and speed away.

The nerve of that man!

Why did all her dates go like this now? Despite getting asked out by countless suitors, not one engaged her in fun conversation or really seemed to like any of the same things she did. Not one made her voice catch or her heart skip a beat. Not one felt compelling enough for Ellie to agree to their offers of second dates.

At least none of them had tried to force themselves on her though... well, until tonight. Ugh, he'd been the worst one yet, giving her little hope that she would ever find—and managed to hold onto—*the one*.

She sighed loudly and leaned back in her seat as she navigated her car back onto the freeway. The rain that poured outside matched her suddenly dark mood.

Why does dating have to be so hard? Ellie Hawkins knew she was a catch by anyone's standards. In fact, she'd been named as one of the hottest celebs under thirty by a major industry magazine earlier that month. Yes, her star was on the rise, and soon she'd have more money than she knew what to do with. People often referred to her as this generation's Brooke Shields, which made it easy to book one job after the next, made it easy to succeed in the cutthroat world of modeling.

Yes, Ellie had everything going for her...

Everything *except* someone to love her.

Her heart somersaulted as she thought about *him*, the one man she'd let herself love and who she'd once believed actually loved her in return. But her fairytale wasn't meant to have a happy ending after all. That once upon a time love hadn't been willing to be the man she needed—and so they'd ended their relationship a couple months back with broken dreams, broken promises, and two very broken hearts.

But two months felt like an eternity ago now. Ellie was determined she didn't need him, and she was going to prove it to herself by finding a man who *would* fit in her life. She'd find someone who could love her just as she was and just as she deserved.

Until then, unfortunately, it would just be Ellie and her mom.

Yes, Ellie loved her mother, but she honestly couldn't be sure the feeling was mutual. Ever since Ellie was a little girl, her mom had been enrolling her in pageants and traipsing her all over the world for opportunities she had missed for herself and would make darn sure Ellie didn't miss, too.

At first, little Ellie had hated the pageants. She remembered crying and wanting to go home, but her mom never let her give up. She'd spent thousands of dollars on dresses and other accessories Ellie would need to win the top prizes. Her room was now filled with tiaras, crowns, ribbons, and trophies from her years on the pageant circuit. And she'd slowly grown accustomed to the pageants—even if she'd never truly enjoyed them.

Sometimes Ellie still felt like she was racking up Grand Supreme titles as part of her grown-up pageantry. Impress the designer, land the gig, smile, smile, smile, smile. Her mom was still by her side, of course. She'd become the kind of "momager" that could even put Kris Jenner to shame. After all, she only had one child to dote on instead of a whole clan.

But at least she was devoted. Obsessively devoted.

As she transitioned her wipers to high speed, Ellie tried to convince herself that she had everything she needed in her life, that she'd be better off without the man who'd broke her heart. Still, she felt her patience wearing thin. Just how many more miserable dates would she have to go on before she could find someone to help her forget him?

Tears started to blur her vision, so she reached up to wipe at her eyes.

He's not worth it. I already have everything I need.

As Ellie ran through these affirmations in her head, she closed her eyes for the briefest of moments. When she opened them again, she noticed a wet blur streaking across the curved road in front of her.

She noticed, but she barely had the time she needed to react.

The foolish doe had frozen in fear, and if Ellie didn't at least try to do something—and fast—they'd both be goners.

She jerked her steering wheel hard, sending her tires skidding across the flash flood that had begun to pool on the lonely road. The sudden motion startled the deer, sending it running back into the trees at the edge of the road.

Ellie continued to hold her breath as she swung the wheel back around, trying to straighten her vehicle as she'd learned so many years ago in drivers ed. Her tires locked in a hydroplane, letting out a ghastly shriek as machine fought nature...

And lost.

Everything moved in slow motion, and just like that darned deer, Ellie froze. She watched in horror as her trusted car betrayed her, spinning across the road and careening down, down, down.

The giant hunk of metal flipped and twisted around her as they both went over the edge of the road where no guardrail had been placed to prevent their fall.

Clenching her eyes shut, Ellie tightened every muscle in her body as she waited for the impact.

Please, God. Don't let this be the end. She didn't know whether she had spoken her prayer aloud, but either way, she hoped God heard it—and hoped He wasn't too angry with her to intervene and save her from this living nightmare.

The first roll sent Ellie even faster down the edge. Her body slammed against the driver's side door before being hurled back to the other side like a rag doll. Her hands came off the steering wheel and frantically tried to grab onto something to hold as she spun over and over down the ditch.

Suddenly, the vehicle hit a rock, hurling it into the air again before landing with a hard crash onto the roof. Her head slammed into the corner of the window which was now crushed inside, then bounced back to hit the steering wheel in front.

Excruciating pain shot through her body, and a moment of clarity stopped the world around her for the briefest of interludes.

In that moment, she realized that instead of worrying

about whether she'd ever work again, or if she'd suffer some kind of injury that would destroy her modeling career, or even what her mother would think, the only thoughts Ellie had were of *him*, the one who'd gotten away.

The pain taking over her body was nothing compared to the agony crushing her heart.

She already knew she'd never feel his arms around her again or see his whole face light up when he laughed—and, without the promise of a future together, perhaps it wouldn't be worth surviving this crash anyway.

What happens next?
Don't wait to find out...

Read the next two chapters right now in Melissa Storm's free book app.

Or head to my website to purchase your copy so that you can keep reading this sweet, heartwarming series today!

Home Sweet Home

The Sunday Potluck Club

Wednesday Walks and Wags

The Church Dogs of Charleston

A very special litter of Chihuahua puppies born on Christmas day is adopted by the local church and immediately set to work as tiny therapy dogs.

The Long Walk Home

The Broken Road to You

The Winding Path to Love

Alaskan Hearts: Sled Dogs

Get ready to fall in love with a special pack of working and retired sled dogs, each of whom change their new owners' lives for the better.

The Loneliest Cottage

The Brightest Light

The Truest Home

The Darkest Hour

Alaskan Hearts: Memory Ranch

This sprawling ranch located just outside Anchorage helps its patients regain their lives, love, and futures.

The Sweetest Memory

The Strongest Love

The Happiest Place

The First Street Church Romances

Sweet and wholesome small town love stories with the community church at their center make for the perfect feel-good reads!

Love's Prayer

Love's Promise

Love's Prophet

Love's Vow

Love's Trial

Sweet Promise Press

What's our Sweet Promise? It's to deliver the heartwarming, entertaining, clean, and wholesome reads you love with every single book.

Saving Sarah

Flirting with the Fashionista

Stand-Alone Novels and Novellas

Whether climbing ladders in the corporate world or taking care of things at home, every woman has a story to tell.

A Mother's Love

A Colorful Life

Love & War

Do you know that Melissa also writes humorous Cozy Mysteries as Molly Fitz? Click below to check them out:
www.MollyMysteries.com

MEET THE AUTHOR

Melissa Storm is a New York Times and multiple USA Today bestselling author of Women's Fiction and Inspirational Romance.

Despite an intense, lifelong desire to tell stories for a living, Melissa was "too pragmatic" to choose English as a major in college. Instead, she obtained her master's degree in Sociology & Survey Methodology—then went straight back to slinging words a year after graduation anyway.

She loves books so much, in fact, that she married fellow author Falcon Storm. Between the two of them, there are always plenty of imaginative, awe-inspiring stories to share. Melissa and Falcon also run a number of book-related businesses together, including LitRing, Sweet Promise Press, Novel Publicity, and Your Author Engine.

When she's not reading, writing, or child-rearing, Melissa spends time relaxing at her home in the Michigan woods, where she is kept company by a seemingly unending quantity of dogs and two very demanding Maine Coon rescues. She also writes under the names of Molly Fitz and Mila Riggs.

CONNECT WITH MELISSA

You can download my free app here:
melstorm.com/app

Or sign up for my newsletter and receive an exclusive free story, *Angels in Our Lives*, along with new release alerts, themed giveaways, and uplifting messages from Melissa!
melstorm.com/gift

Or maybe you'd like to chat with other animal-loving readers as well as to learn about new books and giveaways as soon as they happen! Come join Melissa's VIP reader group on Facebook.
melstorm.com/group

ACKNOWLEDGMENTS

This one goes out to all the dads, especially those with daughters. It is that special bond that inspired this story and gave it its emotional intensity.

To the dad who chose not to stick around, thus giving me all the angst I needed to one day start writing.

And also to the dad who picked up the slack, who raised me, adopted me, claimed me as his, shared his outlook on the world. Even though we don't always—okay, we *rarely*—agree, I love you, and I'm so thankful to have you in my life.

To my father-in-law who is basically the perfect dad in every way and who raised my own romantic hero into a strong, compassionate man—even though I know a certain Mr. Storm made that incredibly difficult.

To a certain Mr. Storm who shares the greatest gift of all with me, our fabulous daughter, Phoenix. And who is eager to open his home and heart to our future adopted child (I can't wait to meet you, little one!).

To the dad my little brother will soon be. Oh, boy, is your world about to change in ways you can only begin to imagine!

To all the dads who stay, especially when it's hard. And to those who don't, may they find the love they are missing from their lives.

To you, dear reader, and the men in your life—both amazing and less than.

Thank you for inspiring me.

All my love,

Melissa S.

P.S. Oh, yeah! And also to the people who aren't dads but still helped make this book a reality: Megan Harris, Jasmine Bryner, Angi DeMonti, Becky Muth, the Storm Super Readers, and my many, many author friends. Thank you!

Made in the USA
Monee, IL
07 May 2021

68008327R00154